THE LONG MOONLIGHT

RazörFist

The Long Moonlight
Nightvale 1

RazörFist

Published by Dark Legion Books
www.arkhavencomics.com

Cover: Dominuz
Illustrations: Julianne Griepp

ISBN: 978-952-7303-09-2

Contents

To the memory of
Uncle Bruce

For encouragement, even when unsolicited

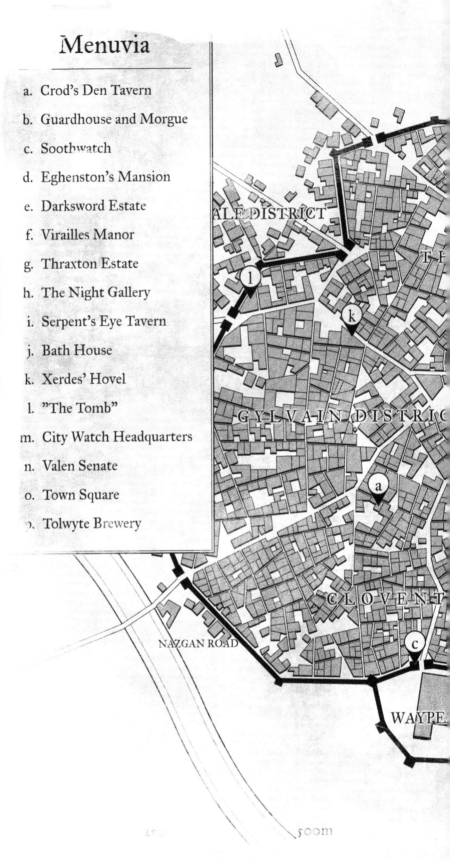

Menuvia

ALE DISTRICT

T. F

GYLVAIN DISTRIC

CLOVENT

NAZGAN ROAD

WAYPE.

500m

Chapter 1
Arson and Avarice

Trisday, 23rd of Ántilián, 1856

The final tumbler fell into place with a dull click.

Xerdes chanced a final glance from beneath his drawn hood to ensure his choice of vocation hadn't been elevated to a spectator sport. Only the looming, obsidian spires of the Menuvian skyline[1] glowered back at

---

[1] Menuvia: Former capital of the twin kingdom of Vale. Though its status was reduced after the Cerulean War, its wealth and influence was not. As a conciliatory gesture, it was allowed to house the Senate. The vast majority of Valen nobles maintain their sprawling mansions in Menuvia, rather than the capital city of Tirionus.

him. Distant torchlights and illuminated windows lay couched on the dark horizon, benign and sightless.

Silence. Or as close an imitation as Menuvia could muster.

At last, he heaved aside the obese, oaken door, the practiced movements of a seasoned sneak ensuring he did so without a sound.

The footfalls that suddenly sounded from the end of the street did not cooperate. It was a rattling, heavy-hoofed staccato. The kind only the clumsiest sentry can manage. A long shadow stretched through the lamplight at the end of the street.

The thief's wraithlike frame melted through the passageway and into the tavern and remained there, frozen in space, for several breathless moments. The footsteps outside grew in volume, the sentry's torchlight casting unearthly shadows that crawled across the inn's wood-paneled walls. The footsteps faded. The building stilled.

All was pitch inside the inn. Not even a pale shaft of moonlight to pierce the velvet shroud.

Xerdes went to work.

Probing his way down what felt like a hollow wooden stoop, his boots at last met stone. If his daytime survey of the premises had proven fruitful—and the ownership hadn't taken up midnight furniture rearrangement as a hobby—there should be a hearth twelve paces or so from the door.

A hearth with a set of fine silver casks on its mantlepiece.

Shuffling in silence across the chilly stone floor, he crept to the opposite wall, his gloved fingers gliding deftly along the edge of the fireplace. One of them stopped.

Xerdes felt the edges of his mouth pull into a smirk.

Even through the soft, lambskin leather of his gloves, it was unmistakable. The cool caress of a silver carafe.

He unclasped a small bag from the rear of his belt and drew its mouth agape. A half-dozen casks in total slid quietly into its deceptive depths, and a quick tug of the drawstring pulled it shut at his side. The rear of the bar made a tempting target, but navigating the obstacle course of empty bottles and silverware he had observed earlier made it a forbidding prospect. Moreover, Xerdes nourished the niggling suspicion—given both the richness of the décor and the proprietor's pronounced High-crest accent—that the man likely kept his oldest vintage on the upper floor, nearer his bed quarters. Xerdes had found men of material wealth often labored under the belief that merely lying unconscious with their valuables caused it to appreciate in value.

Noting their proclivities had become a preoccupation since Xerdes had set up shop in the posh Cloventine District, and while he hadn't done nearly as much mapping of its wards and byways as he perhaps should, it seemed the compulsions of the rich were not unique to his native Gylvain Quarter, where the residents abided in filth and squalor. At this point, the only real difference he'd noted was a more pleasant aroma upon stepping outside.

The thief ceased all movement.

He could hear the faint footfalls sounding in the other direction now. As the torchlight's gleam sent beams of orange light probing the blackness inside, he heard heavy fingers fumbling with a keyring.

Xerdes had company.

He hurriedly scaled the wooden planks of a staircase nestled in the east wall, his silhouetted frame sweeping up to the second floor like a

black vapor, deciding that forsaking the bar on the first floor and all its valuables, for the bigger payout above, was the wiser move. Expert footing elicited nary a creak from the weathered boards, and he quickly ascended to the adjoining upstairs hallway. A shadowy shape, wreathed in weak, silvery moonlight glided down the hallway. Copperware, coins, and other valuables vanished in its ghostly wake.

It paused.

At the far edge of the hallway, he could just make it out. The muffled sound of male voices. One, exceptionally deep, gravelly, very much the dominant force, by the sound of it. The other halting, nervous, perhaps younger by a decade or two. And familiar. As he drew his gaze to the corner the sounds emitted from, he could see the faintest torchlight shuddering through a door. A voyeuristic compulsion drew him near, until Xerdes found his eye aligned with the crack in the doorframe. He saw nothing but a naked wall and the shadow of a man, tied to a chair, with a much larger, oak of a gentleman, hovering above him threateningly. He could hear the gravelly voice, booming from beneath the door.

"...enston is the precise variety of serpent I expect this from. And attempt, to the best of my ability, to anticipate—"

"Oh, aye, sir—"

A sound like a tree branch striking a cliff face cut him off.

Xerdes could hear the man pacing The slats in the floor groaned with his every footfall, betraying his bulk.

"Hiring from the outside was my first mistake." he fumed, "I usually go in-house for a job like this."

His voice then fell to a sinister, throaty growl once more as he pressed on, "You are going to tell me... what you told Rolf Eghenston about my operation." The shadow of the large man gripped his companion by the throat. "...and then you are going to tell me... how you knew a single rutting thing about my business... without me imparting that knowledge to you."

Eghenston!

The name seared through Xerdes' mind. It couldn't be.

The only Eghenston he'd known was long dead. He'd watched Eghenston die.

"T-take it easy, Cy! I-I did manage to find where Eghenston was laying his hea—"

With a loud clatter, the large man kicked his seated companion across the room. Still tied helplessly to the chair, he clattered to the floor and into Xerdes' line of sight.

He thought he'd recognized the waifish voice. The drawn, pale features and unkempt tufts of red hair all confirmed his suspicions. It was Myron Lark, an independent more commonly operating from his very own corner of his old district. Hardly a rival to Xerdes, whose past, and skill, had kept him in reasonably high demand since the fall of the Guilds, but accomplished enough at his handicraft. Lark was a small-time housebreaker and had no doubt misrepresented his abilities to his pugnacious employer in the hope of elevating his station in the suddenly lucrative Menuvian underworld. Power vacuums had a way of doing that.

If Eghenston rang an eerie tone, the name Cy was a dead note. Either way, he was a heavy hitter. A big shot you could spot from five rooftops over. There would be no reason for Xerdes to know him at all. Higher society crime comes with higher stakes, Xerdes reasoned... and if you didn't soar with eagles, you never plummet to the earth.

"Yes, thank you, you parasite! Thank you for following the breadcrumbs my competent agents laid out for you and subsequently locating the corner of operations I could have found myself on an evening stroll! Your powers of perception... are truly a marvel. Now..."

Suddenly, the big man lumbered into frame. A stocky, middle-aged giant with rough-hewn features: head completely shaven to hide his baldness—but failing—and a broad, dark mustache like a pushbroom below a pointed nose. His dark eyes seared like anthracite.

Xerdes heard a tearing sound, as a meaty paw reached down and lifted Myron by his unfastened shirt collar.

"Askin' twice makes me disagreeable."

"J-just told him where I was hired! H-He knows this is your joint."

The lie seemed sound before he said it. Welliver wasn't biting.

"I had a shadow this morning. Seemed to know my routine. Which, paranoid type that I am... I know you ain't privy to..."

"I... I followed you. For a week. From here. F-figured it might be valuable if... if..."

The big man wrapped his fingers around Myron's frail throat.

"Look. Y-you've got a reputation... I n-needed to plan for a double-cross is all!"

Myron Lark was being far too talkative, Xerdes thought to himself. He knew this tune and how it ended for the songbird. Myron had very nearly outlived his usefulness to Cy or whoever he was. Xerdes began to ponder the possibility of intervening. His relationship with the fence was purely professional, but he'd done nothing to deserve a death in a dark tavern.

"I've never known Eghenston to leave an informant alive that didn't give him enough in return to warrant the gesture."

"P-please don't kill me, Mr. Welliver!"

Xerdes froze.

Cyrus Welliver. You didn't have to soar with pigeons, let alone eagles, to spot his influence from the sky. You could spot it on a cloudy day. In an eclipse. While blindfolded.

Xerdes knew Cyrus all right. Xerdes planned to live to a ripe, retiring age by limiting their interactions entirely. That plan wasn't going well at the moment.

Mired in thought and possibility, Xerdes nearly missed the gurgling noises from beyond the door in front of him. Welliver was strangling Myron Lark to death in front of his eyes! As Myron struggled to breathe, Xerdes felt his fingers wrap tightly around the hilt of his dagger. A curved blade of Nazgan[2] make, banded in blued steel. Myron's eyes darted frantically about the room. The fuming goliath seemed to finally take notice of the crack in the door, and the cloaked figure in the dark hallway beyond. The gurgles grew louder as his eyes seemed transfixed on Xerdes.

In a flash, the thief drew his dagger.

---

[2] Nazgan: An arid, coastal country west of Vale. Inhabited by nomadic men of the desert and the treacherous kingdom of the cold-blooded Bords.

'Myron,' he thought to himself, 'I expect a sizeable discount for—'

Just then, the sound of a wooden chair clattering to the stone floor below rang through the entire tavern. Welliver stopped dead, his fingers slipping from Lark's throat. Coughing and sputtering, Myron desperately attempted to regain his wind.

"I'll hand it to Eghenston. The man wastes no time on prelude," Welliver chortled bemusedly. As he reached for a knife sheathed in back of his breeches, Myron began to sputter.

"T-the *hack* ch-check th-the... *coff*... the door!"

Welliver's eyes narrowed as he wheeled to approach the hallway door.

"I-intruder!" Myron choked out on the floor behind him, "W-watchin' the *hack* whole bloody thing! Xer— *coff*..."

Cyrus Welliver's eyes narrowed in dawning realization. He threw wide the door.

Nothing.

An empty, moonlit hallway.

Welliver began to turn when he felt the icy chill of steel pressed to his leathery neck.

"Evening," came the smoky rumble of Xerdes' voice.

"Wish I had five like you," Welliver's eyebrow cocked itself as he raised his chin to make a more tempting target of his throat. "If Eghenston's stock improved this much, I trust you not to bungle the job. I'd rather not bleed out for a fortnight."

"Untie him."

Cy's eyes blinked open. "W-what...?"

"Cut his bonds and leave," whispered Xerdes and with that, kicked the crime lord between his broad shoulders, sending him stumbling in Myron's direction. Welliver's knife came clattering to the floor beside him. By the time Cyrus had parted his face from the floorboards and turned back around, he found Myron Lark to be the only other person in the room.

"Adon's balls..." he muttered. Then, brandishing his knife, he cut Myron free from the chair.

Saryss had reached the top of the stairs when she heard it. A clattering of bottles in the direction of the bar itself. She spun in place to face the sound, her strong features twisted with Horrand fury.

"Dunwyn!" she whisper-screamed. Was the festering inebriate not content with merely stumbling into a door and fouling their element of surprise? She gripped the angular handle of a Horrand broadsword tightly between her hands. It was hardly the instrument of an assassin, but it was a weapon that had served her too well to part with. Hearing nothing in reply, she turned toward the dark corner where the sound had originated. The door closed behind them. The room had now become an inkwell.

"Dunwyn…" she whispered more quietly and crept down the stairs and toward the bar.

Suddenly, she hit the wall. She thought she had been struck. From where?

Her right side. Surely her side.

Another blow came, missing her head by inches. Flinging free her blade, she soon felt a stiff strike to her left elbow, accompanied by a hollow pop. The sword darted from her grasp and plunged into a nearby chair. Her left arm folded at her side, mangled and useless.

The shadow was all around her, striking with ruthless precision.

An easy job. This was supposed to be an easy job.

Her dagger was on the right side, where her shattered arm could not reach. She had one final weapon. A weapon that was to be reserved for disposing of the corpses once Welliver had been slain. She drew the torch from beneath

8

her cloak. The flint slid from her pouch with ease and nestled between her fingers. She made a snapping motion.

Her weapon was light.

Xerdes stood revealed, stern-faced, dagger sheathed. She could see his chiseled features, shadowed by a day or two's growth of beard, a few sienna strands hanging before a pair of firm, confident eyes. His lips crept into a sardonic smirk. Dunwyn's unconscious body lay crumpled in a heap in the far corner of the room. She rightly surmised that her watchman, Athros, had met the same fate outside.

As she held the torch aloft, Saryss watched the smirk subside in dismay. He had clearly not known he was striking a woman. Until now.

If her alabaster complexion, square features, and statuesque frame hadn't marked her as a Horrand, the splash of cobalt warpaint[3] that cut laterally across a pair of pallid azure eyes would have.

Horrands were hardy, barbarian mountain-folk, and even their females were not at all distant from his physical equal. But the prospect of maiming a woman was not one he relished, irrespective of stature. If he allowed her to live, she would give his description to this mysterious Rolf Eghenston. His mind rifled through every permutation of his next move in dizzying seconds.

Saryss's frantic expression suddenly vanished. With a shrug, she cast the torch over her shoulder, where it clattered at the top of the stairs. The boards were dry as sun-bleached driftwood and erupted in flame almost instantly. She dropped to her knees and threw back the hood of her cloak. Pale blonde tresses spilled from beneath her hood, now matted with sweat. Her eyes were shut as she muttered words in a harsh, foreign brogue.

"Kin thjönd möreg."

The one arm she could use slowly stretched toward him in sacrificial abandon. Her eyelids parted halfway, and by the flicker of the firelight

---

[3] Warpaint was once considered a ward against evil in the long past when Göurnoth stood united. In today's clannish era, it holds a fraction of its original meaning, and is often worn by almost anyone of Horrand blood that is aware they may be entering combat. Be they soldiers, mercenaries, or even pirates.

that was swiftly surrounding them both, he could make out a catatonic gaze in a pair of eyes like blue steel.

"You Horrands and your theater..." Xerdes chuckled wryly.

He struck her violently in the face with the hilt of his dagger. Saryss folded sideways on the tavern's stonework.

Through the crackling around him, he heard the roof timber beginning to groan.

"Well, we've certainly had the drama," Xerdes opined in silence. "Time to exit, stage right."

With his bag of ill-gotten haul already cooling in an adjacent storm drain outside, Xerdes had only to exit via the front door. A flash of silvery steel dazzled the periphery of his vision, however. The woman's sword still lay embedded in the seat of a chair feet from her senseless body. His greed briefly overcoming his survival instinct, Xerdes clasped the hilt and drew it free.

Given a thieves' split-second appraisal, it was a work of exceptional craftsmanship. It was no common soldier's blade. The weapons of Göurnoth were better renowned for their utility than their aesthetics, yet the blade's hilt bore knotwork intaglios, and the base of the blade itself was dotted with Ägrigör runes. It was cumbersome perhaps, particularly to a man of his slight build. But it was an item of tremendous value regardless. He sheathed the blade in his belt and prepared to exit.

Yet he found that he still stood in place.

His eyes transfixed on the unconscious Horrand woman. A wooden plank toppled in flame at the stairs behind him with a thunderous crash, yet his gaze remained unshaken.

"A thief with a conscience," he muttered to himself. "Oh, I'll go far..."

Xerdes crouched on a nearby terrace, watching as fiery tendrils roared from the tavern's windows and belched fetid plumes of smoke into the frigid Menuvian night. In cold conscription, it was not so unsuccessful a fracas for the young thief. He had come away with a bulging bag of valuable loot, gained considerably more insight into the city's dangerous patrician underworld, and even enjoyed a fleeting moment with one of the most powerful figures in all of Vale, criminal or otherwise. Better still, his one-time fence had apparently lived to commit further life-threatening errors. It was a resounding victory, generally speaking.

As the cloaked frame of Xerdes vaulted to the adjacent rooftop and prepared to make the long journey back to his quarters in the Gylvain, he stepped to the edge and briefly hesitated.

A resounding victory indeed, he intimated internally—save one, lone indulgence.

Xerdes vaulted from the roof and vanished into the dawn.

Saryss awoke to a skull that seemed committed to the principle of escaping her scalp. Yet even though she was immobilized by waves of violent pain, her first thought was of her compatriots. Crashing through a wall of agony, she managed to briefly rise and take stock of her surroundings. She lay in a slick alleyway of cobbled stone, cattycorner from the tavern she had evidently found her way from—a tavern now more accurately described as smoldering rubble. To her bewilderment, her hazed vision could just make out her fellow assassins, Athros and Dunwyn, folded neatly against the very wall she was now propped against, still giddily unconscious.

"Drögnän's cock!" she abruptly gasped. For her sheath lay empty at her side. Her sword taken, the fogged moors of her memory were beginning to clear.

"Sh-shtop shoutin', will ye'?" she heard Dunwyn mumble as he slowly began to stir from unconsciousness.

"Well, if it isn't the Muddled Mercenary!" she exclaimed venomously. "Good of you to rejoin the conscious."

"T-take i' easy, will ye?" he slurred, "Between being knocked out an' the 'angover, it feels like a hyperactive blacksmiff is poundin' ore in me 'ead."

"One sunrise and one assault later and still somehow shitfaced. What fortune for Rolf to have paired us. Obviously, Welliver hired outside protection. Scrawny bastard made off with Gjörgen Khäl..."

"Nonsense!" Dunwyn bellowed. "I'm certain your cowl will turn up!"

"My sword, Crodshit! Where I come from, our weapons have a name. And a soul. We pass them from generation to generation. To steal a clan-sworn weapon warrants execution. If I still had use of my sword ar—" she stopped dead.

Her shattered arm.

It had been set and wrapped in bandages.

Cyrus Welliver hacked and wheezed his way down a steamy, cobbled alleyway. He had run for nearly two blocks, Myron Lark stumbling through the seedy Menuvian side streets just a few paces ahead. Without warning, both men collapsed, nearly in unison, having ducked into the small garden of an oblivious nobleman.

Myron at last broke the succession of labored gasps with an expression of the obvious.

"Th-they aren't following us."

Welliver, lying on his back in a bed of foliage, replied only with an exasperated glance.

"Well, I should. . ."

Cy's meaty paw smacked against Myron's neck before he could utter another word.

"That. . . man. . ." he hoarsely wheezed.

"Th-the intruder?"

"The. . . very same."

"J-just looked like an independent, to me. . . probably not one of Eghenston's—"

"Assuredly. . . not." Cy agreed, his breath beginning to slow. "Which is why you have one last thing to give me before I give your sad story an end. . ."

Myron Lark choked back sobs as the mammoth Cy Welliver hovered above him.

"His name."

Chapter 2
The Violet Veil

Fallday, 25th of Ántilián, 1856

Even before his feet had touched the floorboards, Xerdes knew.

All was not as it should be in his hovel.

Though the intruder had left no apparent sign of his presence, to a practiced sneak, the room bore all the atmospheric hallmarks of intrusion. Sounds traveled differently, even the wind, little more than a hushed whisper at his back, wound throughout the room more reservedly when a foreign entity lurked within. He silently heaved through the windowsill, a shaft of pale blue moonlight casting his long, cloaked shadow across the room. A gloved hand warily hovered before the hilt of his dagger as he addressed the darkness.

"If house-breaking is your game, intruder, you'll find the storm drains outside more profitable than this humble shitbox."

The shadows seemed to ponder his words before replying.

"All I seek is a moment of your time," the shadows whispered in reply.

"I don't converse with the invisible."

An ephemeral spark flitted in the far corner of the room, preceding the dull glow of an oil lantern. A massive hand, clad only in a tapered leather gauntlet, deposited the lamp on Xerdes' dining room table. The stranger stood, now fully illuminated by the gloomy lamplight.

"'Member me, mate?" the stranger said.

Xerdes let out a bemused sigh and settled into a nearby chair.

"The assassin."

Dunwyn's mouth pulled into a toothless grin.

"One of 'em. Yes."

Xerdes suddenly realized his implication, but before he could wheel about and stand, he felt a cold blade press its way to the nape of his neck. A lean arm pinned his elbows behind his back and pulled him up from his seat. Before the words came rolling from her lips, the pallid blonde ringlet that spilled onto his shoulder revealed his captor's identity.

"You have taken something of mine, thief," Saryss whispered through clenched teeth. "A weapon to which I am honor-bound. My Gjörgen Khäl."

Her scent teased his nose. Like rose petals on hemlock.

Xerdes felt his mouth pull into a smirk.

"If you'd been this good a sneak to begin with, you may never have parted with—"

—he felt the business end of the blade press emphatically against the base of his skull.

"The time for bartering is past," hissed the Horrand maiden. "And even were it not, yours is a poor bargaining position indeed."

Xerdes took in the room. Wary eyes, those of a seasoned cutpurse, keen to opportunity even in the direst of circumstance, darted across every crevice of his domestic squalor. Across the dusty table, Dunwyn had settled, smug and self-satisfied, caressing the length of his crossbow and eyeing him expectantly. In a far corner smoldered Athros, still seething from being taken unaware two nights previous. Wiry of frame and of dusky complexion, he might have been mistaken for a poorly watered houseplant were it not for the half-drawn short sword at his belt. Xerdes' eyes swept over his cloaked figure. They came to rest in the corner opposite, just beside a bulbous wood stove, bristling with rivets that wept with rust.

"You'll never last, you know. In this line of work," the thief said with a knowing sigh.

Athros, transfixed upon Xerdes' face, had noted his eyes lingering near the stove. He began to traverse the room, considering every floorboard warily.

"I've known many an assassin, m'lady—"

"Do not take your tone with me as a familiar, blaggard," she spat. "You know precious little of me or my profession."

Athros knelt down near the stove, his fingered gloves groping the timber in the walls along the corner suspiciously. Xerdes' eyes narrowed as he bandied with his captor, whose blade seemed destined to meet his brain.

"Oh, no argument on that score, madame," he chuckled, "Of you and your people, I know precious little. You keep indoors, swilling mead in your mountain halls in the south..."

At this insult, he felt her grasp the side of his drawn hood with her free hand, taking what felt like a tuft of hair with it. Evidently, she was a patriot. He tried not to ponder the excitement this act of sadism caused him. He had, after all, paid good money to Menuvian whorekeeps for similar treatment. And, to be blunt, none of those women was nearly as well-proportioned.

"...but of your profession?" he continued, "you don't move in my circles without brushing up against at least one..." he paused, momentarily amused by the serendipity of his word choice with the physics of his current predicament, "...cutthroat."

Xerdes heard her scoff derisively. In the corner, Athros was all but pressed to the floor, his fingers sweeping across a particular group of planks. He'd seen blood-starved rifthounds less committed to the hunt.

"If this is all you know of my trade, thief," she leaned in, her mouth nearly pressed to his face so that he could feel her breath playing across his ear, "...stick to judging my ethnicity. At least it's only conventionally insulting."

Athros purred in the corner, a low, throaty rumble, indicating he'd found something. He sat erect with a start, both gloved hands feeling for a catch on either side of the wooded floor-planks, and with a hearty heave given his frame, he began to pull. The floor was unimpressed. A low grunt in Dunwyn's direction persuaded his accomplice to quit his seat at the table to help Athros to pull the lid loose on what he now imagined to be a lucrative thieves' bounty secreted within.

"Very well," Xerdes mused, settling back in mock-comfort against Saryss' knife blade. "You're a clannish people. Hardy. Warlike and peace-loving all at once. Your men can stand as much as two heads above we lowly manfolk, even at average..."

The two burglars clutched at the floorboards in abject futility, lacking any conceivable leverage to pull it loose, first taking turns, and finally coordinating their fruitless efforts. Yet still the secret compartment, the outline of which could now plainly be seen, refused to yield.

"...you have a love of song, snow, and sleet. Of warm halls and light-hearted fellowship. Most impressively of all, to me? Good, brown ale. You bend knee to no King, but your Firth—let's be honest, m'lady; a glorified warlord—is feared by all just the same. For why would any people with such singular focus need a crown to bring them to heel...?"

Athros looked up from his frustrated efforts, seeming to take note of the rust-bespeckled furnace for the first time. Indicating to Dunwyn, they each braced a foot against its metallic bulk and heaved backward with all their might. The wooden lid came free with an abrupt pop, erupting in a hail of dust, lit full in the single shaft of moonlight from the nearby window.

"O-ho!" crowed Dunwyn, " 'Ave a look 'ere! A li'l leather bundle o' some sort."

Athros sneezed violently, unable to peer down at what his partner had indicated. Saryss gave them a momentary nod and tightened her grip on the helpless thief, more preoccupied with his acknowledgement of their victory than the actual achievement of it.

Xerdes continued, unperturbed. His boots slowly arcing up to rest against the front legs of his dining room chair. "...the only force to ever truly put the Empire to rights? To sack our cities or put them to the torch? That takes focus. Unbending. Unflinching. Complete absorption in one thing..."

Dunwyn hoisted the leather bag atop the stove, ribbons of dust, luminous in the moonlight, bellowing in all directions as he did so. From within, he produced a silver carafe. Eating utensils. Plates. A respectable haul, but with no sword and nothing of greater value at hand, he thought it a decoy.

Until he felt something else at the bottom of the bag. Reaching deeply, almost up to his shoulder, Dunwyn felt his hand wrap around a perfectly round, spherical object, utterly smooth to the touch.

...and then he felt that object shatter.

A low hiss emanated from the bag, as clouds of black smoke, accented with deepest purple billowed from its unseen depths. The stench of an abattoir, intermingled with a fragrance of deepest lavender, at once permeated the air. Dunwyn, having taken one breath of the substance, went immediately rigid and collapsed, his limbs twitching violently.

Saryss' eyes shot open, as if from a trance. "Traps! It's a bloody decoy!"

Athros started for the window, but plumes of purple, as if sentient, overtook him, and he was at once reduced to a gibbering, twitching mass, huddled against the windowsill.

"...one thing and nothing else," Xerdes finished with a single chuckle. And he kicked the front legs of his chair out from under himself, causing him to topple forward to the floor, away from his assailant's blade, his forehead missing the table's edge by inches. Saryss, still reeling from the sudden reversal, failed to catch him. In one fluid motion, Xerdes brushed his hand along the bottom of the table. Probing. Groping. Grabbing the handle of a cold, steel dagger nailed to its undercarriage. That same motion had shifted the table, knocking the lamp at its edge to the floor and plunging the entire room into darkness, save the single shaft of moonlight, with Athros' frame just visible, convulsing and writhing like a dying insect just at its feet.

The Horrand blood in Saryss's veins—hardened as it is against the frigid elements—ran like ice water. Her allies were convulsing in what might well be their death throes, envenomed by an unknown, fell magic, and somewhere in the inky shadows of his very own abode... lay her newly-escaped quarry, and as sure as she had heard a dagger being drawn from a sheath secreted beneath the table mere moments ago...? He was now armed as well.

"If we're to keep meeting like this..." she heard him snicker from all directions at once, "at some point, we're due a proper introduction."

"Saryss of Yüetagosomb, thief. Learn it. Because until you return my lifeblade, that name will labor your every breath."

"Nice name. They pay the guy who thought of it by the letter?"

"Darkforge to you, human," she spat. "Saryss of Darkforge."

'The Horrand capital?' he mused in silence. She thought she heard the groan of a wooden plank at her back. The cold blade being drawn across her neck from behind told Saryss her hearing was in working order. Xerdes' hand slowly worked its way down her bodice to check for

weapons. It lingered playfully over body parts he particularly appreciated. "Wouldn't have pegged you for a city girl." He drew his gloved hand across her body and indicated to the writhing forms of Dunwyn and Athros, "Conducting that sideshow, you stick out like a python on a spring roll."

The amaranthine mist still hung in thick plumes over what she now assumed were her friends' corpses. Far from dissipating, it had begun to slowly encroach upon their position. Her steely cerulean eyes shot wide in dread.

"If I'm to perish, I'd just as soon you had the balls to do it yourself," she growled, the Horrands' ancestral fear of magic thick in her throat. "Even being dispatched from behind by a coward is more honorable a death than whatever that... abomination is..."

She felt him pull in tighter behind her. Now it was Xerdes' lips pressed to her ear.

"The Violet Veil," he whispered, "...is a discriminating killer. Or so I'm told. I read up on it a bit after I... acquired it from Soothwatch Tower[1] some two years ago. Always read the instructions..."

The veil had engulfed the entirety of Saryss' right calf. The scent of brimstone and lavender played at her nostrils.

"Odd marks, mages. Not much gold to speak of, but on the table was a velvet bag... and a book opened to some... ancient gibberish about a man-eating mist that suffocates everything in its path... but only feeds on fear..."

The Violet Veil danced around her thighs, now, billowing upward. Xerdes, curiously, appeared unmoved at her back.

"Humane sort that I am," she felt his blade fall from her neck, but the gesture was purely ceremonial. Escape was now impossible. The cloud was paralytic upon contact. Her legs were numbed and rigid, the muscles of her thighs drawn taut as boat-rigging. A cold, necrotic sensation coursed through the lower half of her body. Xerdes continued leisurely, "I figured 'who would be more afraid... than someone burglarizing a fellow thief?' And lo," she watched him back away and hook his leg over the windowsill, a long, sackcloth bundle slung across his shoulder. "...my alarm system was born. Quick, efficient, lethal to those who earn it, and best of all...?"

The veil was lapping over her breasts and up to her neck even as he withdrew.

"...dangerous only to those with enough curiosity and greed... to open the bag."

As he was about to step fully through the window, Saryss saw him hesitate. He pulled off the long, rigid bundle and tossed it in her direction.

---

[1] Soothwatch Tower: Home of The Beholden, the reclusive circle of magi in Vale.

She heard it clatter to the floor, but her neck refused to bend to actually see what it was.

"You know that legendary Horrand bloodwrath you feel boiling up right about now…?"

Her eyes could only narrow to icy slits of blue venom.

"Hold on to it. You might survive."

She saw Xerdes' hooded silhouette dive from the window frame into nebulous night… and then the world was subsumed by a cloud of violaceous dread… and Saryss saw no more.

Inspector Coggins had a mind of clockwork and ice. Where most would dismiss a simple tavern fire as an inevitable hazard of life in a stifling city, Coggins instead pored over the embers for motive. While the sallow-faced, middle-aged guardsman ran a gauntleted hand through mounds of smoldering ash, his clockwork mind overflowed with a labyrinthine knotwork of possibility.

"A wooden building," began his cold appraisal, "incommensurate with the neighborhood. The only tavern in the whole of the Cloventine quarter constructed of such. And for so affluent an establishment. Cyrus Welliver is among th—"

"Welliver is a victim, Inspector," Captain Bevens was less than impressed, cutting his subordinate off before he could even raise from his knees. A vein emerged from his impeccably shorn skull.

He nearly ran his hand through the coarse trim of his graying goatee but caught himself mid-retort. "It's yours to establish whether he is a victim of deliberation or unhappy circumstance. I expect a determination by morning. Consult Sorn[2] on your own time."

Coggins was unswayed, not even turning his uniform gaze from the hypnotic throb of the still-quieting embers. Bevens was a bureaucrat. The recent restructuring of the Menuvian Guard hierarchy made him answerable to senate subcommittees and nobles. Senators were fond

---

[2] Sorn: The long-slumbering Valen god of flame.

of terse, decisive answers devoid of speculation or nuance. And often, thereby, fact. Coggins knew better than to believe he shared the captain's obligations.

He sank a leather-soled boot into one of the cooler patches, pushing charred, skeletal planks from his path as he did so. Just as before. Some torched glass containers and ceramics. No apparent deaths. But no melted or charred metals. Where were the pitchers? The plates? The quintessential tavern paraphernalia?

Coggins had found himself in the Cröd's Den Tavern on just one occasion, for a fellow guardsman's wake. Excluded as he so often was from civil or personal conversation, it had been his purview, instead, to observe. He'd been awed by the furnishings, his mind recalling with crystalline precision row upon row of silver decanters, golden candelabras, and lush Aven[3] tapestries hauled to Menuvia from the distant north at incalculable expense. From the outside, it was a pastiche. A log cabin with a beer tap. Yet the exterior modestly belied its opulence.

Where were the charred or melted remnants of those riches among the rubble? And where, with a staff of nearly a half-dozen, many of whom were reputed to live on the premises... were the bodies?

Narrow black eyes caught sight of something among the hissing planks. It had a handle.

He gripped the haft with a gauntleted hand, and it came free from the ashen ruin with relative ease. It was a length of wood no longer than a fireman's axe... and as he turned it to the side, even with the slightest pressure... granules of blackest charcoal dust tumbled from the far end. His eyes widened in realization but never wavered. He held the remains of a torch—not the recessed variety affixed to tavern walls but the makeshift sort, useful for circumnavigating a cave or a wine cellar.

...or for arson.

Coggins was just rising when a fresh-faced guardsman whose job it had been to secure the scene approached from the adjoining street.

---

[3] Aven: Meaning of, or relating to, the winged Aviári people. Known for their refinement, craft, and increasingly their isolation, they dwell in the northernmost mountainous country of Highcrest.

"Lieutenant, sir!" the wide-eyed law enforcement foundling fumbled, "th-they said the Captain had gone back to—"

"What have you found, Friedrich?" Coggins calmed him with a hand-wave and an even tone.

"We have... that is, sir... we've found a corpse."

Coggins pushed past the equivocating recruit, the trim of his Guard tunic billowing in the sweltering ruins. He'd come in search of evidence and found only questions among the dying flames. If the side streets held answers, Coggins would find them.

Chapter 3
Lethal Liaisons

Maiday, 26th of Ántilián, 1856

Any man resourceful enough to commit arson on the abode of a rival ganglord, rob the rubble clean, and unleash the arsonists on a suspected intruder was a wealthy man indeed.

It just so happened Xerdes was short on wealth. The small fries hadn't fetched much, particularly without Myron Lark in operation. Lark was known for friendly rates, which, in fence terms meant he shot you a mirthful smile as he slid the dagger between your ribs. It beat the bottom-feeders he'd sold the silverware to.

Xerdes had been tempted to ask for payment in string. Then, at least, he could admire the spectacle of being asked if he'd accept half a string.

The reputed crime lord Eghenston was not particularly difficult to locate. With Welliver's operation reduced to cinders, it was a simple matter of trailing one of the usual operators to the only source of dirty money in Menuvia. His quarry didn't make it hard.

Seven heads tall, lumbering and dull witted, Delfin had not been hired for sharpness of mind but bluntness of fist. The apotheosis of hired thug, despite his evident obliviousness, Xerdes granted him an admittedly wide berth as he shadowed the heavy-footed hireling.

The winding, incongruous boulevards of the Gylvain Quarter, where he had first picked up the man-troll's trail, soon gave way to the more orderly, blocky and regimented avenues of the Cloventine District. He hadn't parted company with the patrician district on happy terms and didn't relish the thought of a return, but exigency altered his travel arrangements. Proper cobblestone streets as well as prodigious marble and stone structures imposed at either side. In contrast to the bustle of the squalid markets of the Gylvain, with its ceaseless crush of aberrant humanity and parade of discount market stalls, the sparse opulence of the

Cloventine offered precious little cover. Here, the patricians preferred to charter servants to do their haggling, and thus the stream of mankind was reduced to a modest trickle.

The waning daylight sent shadows sprawling eastward across the becalmed byways of upper class Menuvia. Xerdes melted from one to the next, a spectral nightwraith in his element. If Delfin had chanced a look over his shoulder, he would have sworn the streets abandoned.

The giant lurched to a halt. Xerdes had pulled himself to a higher vantage, perched atop a stone wall draped in rivulets of pale, veridian ivy. A swift glance at his colossal quarry found him dwarfed by the immensity of the estate towering above him. At four stories, it was a testament to the masterful masonwork of a bygone era, when the Horrands, and their seemingly inborn mastery over stone were not so foreign a sight.

Thus located, Xerdes waited shrewdly for the street to quiet and then stole silently, gracefully across the rooftops to his destination. It was a challenge, for so imposing an edifice was Rolf's mansion that no nearby roof or tree loomed over his property. Far from the verdant courts of a true nobleman's estate, Rolf's was a dead and decaying thing, a magnificent structure jutting from thirsty earth and withered foliage.

The seasoned thief dropped at last into the estate's central courtyard, feeling his way about the wall for a hitch. No crime lord worth his weight in bootlegged liquor or narcotic powder would be caught without a hidden entrance, for utilitarian purposes if nothing else.

Yet even as the thief fumbled for a fingerhold on what was fast proving a profoundly solid brick wall, he looked down and saw it. A cellar door, jutting a few inches from the earth.

And quite unlocked.

He pulled the surprisingly thick door up from the Earth and swept beneath the foundations of the mansion with a wordless flourish.

Even with years of hard-earned experience cracking mansions and burglarizing patricians, the familiar feeling inevitably washed over him upon achieving intrusion. The heightened awareness. The prevailing dread. Mingled with the near-intoxication of knowing his continued anonymity hinged wholly on his skill and perception, hereafter. He stole further into a cellar, only the dullest lamp light at the far corner of the room to illuminate his path. Rows upon rows of what looked like exotic wines and liquors becradled in wooden shelving cast shadowy crisscrosses upon his stealthily advancing frame, providing unwitting camouflage for the cutpurse's approach.

He didn't appreciate being burglarized, and using the Violet Veil on such small potatoes seemed a waste of some magnitude. Someone had to pay. And Eghenston could afford the bill.

A cellar staircase, so cold that he could feel it through the soles of his boots, led Xerdes up to the first floor, where the sprawling majesty of the mansion came yawning into view. It was less a home than a cathedral to crime. Milk-white marble pillars sprawled to the arched ceiling, painstakingly scrawled frescoes adorning the entire expanse from wall to ceiling, and at regular intervals, depressions in the wall—where a more religiously inclined structure might affix an icon of Vale's long-dead Gods—hung tokens of his criminal conquests. There were swords of vanquished foes, ornaments purloined through ill-gotten circumstance, and even a bust he recognized: the whiskered visage of Wulf Eghenston, whom he was now all but certain was in some way related to Rolf.

The original thief prince of Menuvia, long-dead.

Xerdes knew, for he had witnessed the deed.

Just as the sneakthief's thoughts began to wander afield of the present, a subtle sound jolted him back to coherence. It was barely perceptible to the untrained ear, but to a larcenist of Xerdes' vintage, it was a portent of doom.

He heard the near-silent slide of brick on brick.

It was a unmistakable prelude to the triggering of a boobytrap. He'd wandered too far into Rolf Eghenston's cavern of criminality... and hadn't yet troubled himself to look down. The tile at his feet, carved into a blood-red ceramic mosaic of what he assumed was the Eghenston family crest, had given way. Before he had a chance to wonder what form the snare would take, he felt it.

A sharp and jolting pain shot up his side, just above his right hip. A clockwork launcher, unseen until triggered, had embedded a projectile in his lower rib. He tore it out instinctively, and what seemed a small throwing knife clattered to the richly appointed floor as Xerdes whirled to the far wall and pressed himself there. The sound of steel missiles sang a lethal euphony at his back, and he at last pressed into the adjoining corridor, presuming the traps were confined to the fresco-laden walls of the Great Hall.

He was wrong, of course.

For the mansion was neither unoccupied nor soundproof. And the clattering of metal on tile carries far in a structure of marble, particularly a monolith such as this. Already, at the far end of the dim hallway, the silhouette of an approaching guardsman could be seen, calling indistinct queries from mere yards' remove.

The thief had not only absentmindedly triggered a trap of the variety that had killed lesser practitioners of his trade, but he had also unknowingly trapped himself.

To Xerdes' rear was a flat marble wall. To his side was the cavernous hall with the arched front doorway bolted at its back. And approaching with sword drawn, and surprising speed, was a guard inquisitive for the wrong reasons. His opportunity narrowing and his options few, the thief would have to act with immediacy.

As the boots of the bewildered guard sounded mere feet away, Xerdes leapt into action.

"Xerdes," the crime baron purred. Cy Welliver sipped in silence for a moment, ruminating on the name. As the mug fell from his lips, a light foam clung to his whiskered mouth. "Who hired a common filcher to—"

"There's no proof 'e was, sir," his slow-witted companion called back from across the tavern table. Though the wreckage of his former headquarters likely still smoldered, Cy suffered no shortage of alternate venues. As a hub of criminality went, he far preferred the informal climes of a pub or tavern. The Serpent's Eye Inn, one of his many semi-legitimate concerns in the Gylvain district, was legitimate enough to turn the prying eyes of any guardsman he didn't presently possess... yet practical enough to his purposes that anyone and everyone had pretext to sup there in secret or otherwise. As headquarters went, it was without peer.

Welliver shot a surprised look in his companion's direction, as if he'd entered the Pub in total secrecy and only now revealed himself. Gollick was a putrid pillbug of a man with small eyes set in a balding, oversized skull. Relative to his round, diminutive frame and shoddy dress, he mightn't have been out of place scrawled on a cave wall from a mixture of dried blood and bird droppings.

He paused to chew on his statement for a moment regardless.

"That," he began with a labored pause, as if forcing the admission from his throat, "...may be the first correct thought you've voiced in the last hour."

Gollick discarded the insult in favor of the compliment. His face lit up like a beetle on a dung pile. His imposing companion continued.

"Why would an independent thief torch my joint when he could leave it standing and return for repeat visits?" He took another long drink and then set the mug down forcefully. His whiskers pulled across a roguish smile, "...until I cut his throat for him, that is."

Gollick's sparsely toothed mouth splayed wide in juvenile glee at the merest suggestion of violence. It was like peering down at an open-faced piano. After a run-in with a sledgehammer. "I've no doubt 'e would've done jus' that, sir—"

"The question of who still confounds me," Cy soldiered on, heedless of his companion's blatherings. "Eghenston agreed to the Night Truce[1]. Proposed it, in fact. He was always the smart one, or so I thought. No one else has the organization. Anyway—"

Welliver lit his pipe while making a vague gesture to a small, flat wooden box at the far end of the table. Gollick immediately fetched it for the big shot. Even an inveterate lackwit sometimes guesses correctly. Welliver drew from the box a single roughshod sheet of paper, scrawling as he muttered aloud to his slow but spellbound companion. "—just because he didn't engineer the arson... doesn't mean he didn't see who did."

---

[1] Night Truce: In late 1838, a gang war over rare Gray Pearls allegedly stolen by Welliver, from rival Rolf Eghenston, hit its apex. A formal armistice between organizations ushered in a golden era for organized crime. The Menuvian black market was thus born, and has thrived ever since.

The writing abruptly stopped, and he reached for two objects. One, a stick of wax, he thrust into the flame of a sputtering candle before them, and the other, Gollick soon came to realize was a stamp.

"...or that anyone is handing out free pardons for robbing my joint."

Cy removed the wax from the flame and pressed the stamp to form a seal. Gollick's eyes went from beads to buttons.

"Th-that's the seal of the—"

"The Menuvian Guard, Gollick."

"Here, sir? Where? I've warrants out in—"

"The seal of the Menuvian Guard, you dolt." He handed the letter to the corpulent pawnbroker and added, "Don't bother telling me you don't know the way to prison. No need to go back the same way you did last time. I doubt your sister is in the mood."

Gollick was dumbfounded. When he at last marshalled his meager faculties, he inquired with uncharacteristic innocence, "What are you planning on doing, sir...?"

"My civic duty, Gollick." Welliver sank back into his bench and took a long drag off his pipe. "Reporting a crime."

———

Xerdes's logic had seemed foolproof mere moments ago.

The sellswords he'd evaded at his former home had been more out for blood than a blade, stolen or otherwise. It was best to follow up on the development and discern what they'd learned about his acquisitive activities.

That, and anyone connected enough to immolate the headquarters of a noted criminal big shot and survive the experience would doubtless be insultingly wealthy.

But now, suspended from the hallway ceiling, a guard mere inches from his back beneath him, with the merest drop of blood from the wound at his side plummeting to the baffled cutthroat below being the only thing between himself and a deadly finish? His logic seemed flawed somehow.

Xerdes felt the air thicken with his presence.

Distance running was clearly not part of Eghenston's audition process. After the guard's exhaustive ten-second jog from the opposite end of the hallway, the brute was wheezing asthmatically like a dying horse. He wheeled to and fro, on vigilant lookout for the vague shadow that had momentarily eluded him.

Xerdes dared not even breathe. Digging his boots into each corner of the wall, pinning himself to the ceiling like a cornered spider was taxing every muscle in his body. Even as lean as he was—a beneficial attribute in his profession—he felt at any moment, his knees or upper body would buckle at the agonizing effort.

The guard paused there beneath him, a long-dormant intellect straining beneath the weight of both his limited faculties and the curious circumstances presented to him.

A pregnant pause followed. Moments became months. Xerdes' elbows and knees began to tremble to the point of exertion as the back of his right heel began to slowly slip down the side of the wall.

"Riftspawn," he heard him scoff, in a thick, slurred Blackcroft[2] accent.

Then, suddenly, the guard whirled in the opposite direction, muttered an inaudible curse, and began the long walk to the opposite end of the hallway, assured it had been a phantom of his own invention.

Xerdes' head never left his shoulder. His eyes followed the guard like an owl over a mousehole as he slowly reached the end of the hallway and at last vanished behind a corner. Only then did Xerdes dismount his precarious vantage and land—with a near-silence born of peerless acrobatic skill—upon the sparsely carpeted marble floor.

His calves and biceps burned like magma beneath his skin as he spun to a shadowy alcove, and he allowed himself to recover his bearings. Xerdes allowed himself only a moment's respite to tear a length of cloth from his tunic to staunch his small stabwound, for the information—and the wealth—he'd come for was doubtless farther in.

Shadowing the very hallway path he'd seen the guard take, Xerdes pressed deftly against the periodic depressions on either side: convex outcroppings that proper patricians would often adorn with ta-

---

[2] Blackcroft: City in the snow-capped Agrigör mountains, far to the southeast of Menuvia. Though occupied largely by Men, Horrands once dwelt there in such abundance that residents are still known for their thick, Göurnoth-tinged accents.

pestries, suits of armor, and other ornaments of their economic station.

Their utter barrenness made Xerdes uneasy as he made his advance though they provided ideal cover.

Passing the hallway he'd seen the guard disappear into, at length, Xerdes came to narrow marble stairs and found his legs still alarmingly unsteady as he ascended to the second floor. The second floor was no more populated than the first. Even peeking in the occasional wooden door offered little more than scarcely appointed rooms and crackling fireplaces.

The fireplaces, too, made him uneasy. Unless they were tended by the wind, that meant servants.

And then he saw it.

An arched passage, teeming with florid green regalia. Verdant tapestries spilling over marble pillars, opening into a vast expanse, rivaling even the size of the great hall near the mansion's entrance.

Golden heraldry wound its way past painted knotwork pillars, stretching to a windowed ceiling above. Gaping at its opulence, Xerdes felt his knees again buckle at the unbridled immensity. A set of silver daggers lined either side of the wall, with silver shields set with ebony between each. He'd no room for the shields, but his knapsack would accommodate the blades nicely. His fatigued footwork failed to hinder him as he was now well apprised of the presence of traps. He took only the lightest steps and paused for even the faintest sound before and after each. At one point, the toes of his boots had scarcely made contact with the floor when he heard the telltale signs of a trap rigging into place, so he withdrew instantaneously.

A projectile screamed across the front of his face as he flew back, nearly pulling one of the unruly tufts of hair peeking from beneath his cloak along with it, missing his head by mere inches.

Fortunately, the dart sank into a richly carven cabinet on the opposite end of the hall, and faintly a sound was made. Sidestepping the snare, Xerdes wound his way to the wall, pulling each dagger free of its mount in sequence, craning paranoically for the sound grinding clockwork or primitive machinery locking in place. The prelude to instant death for many the unripe robber. He heard nothing, as his practiced, catlike movements guided the craftsmanlike blades into his bag with nary a noise. They were half-weapon, half-artwork—flowing Aven blades, with acid-etched embellishments weaving their way from pommel to hilt. His vision nearly blurred at their brilliance, reflected in the shafts of late-afternoon light that spilled through the ceiling. His weakened arms still slightly trembled, but experience allowed him to retain control and ply his trade in sustained silence.

Feline footwork allowed him to all but flow to the opposite wall and do precisely the same. Though the burning sensation was still working its way down his legs. He wondered momentarily when it would abate, when it dawned on him that the sensation was not emanating from his legs... but from his side.

The precise location where the throwing knife had struck. He pressed his hands to the site, and while the stream of blood had all but staunched itself, he could feel it throb and radiate heat even from between his gloves.

Realization dawned on even his chemically muddled mind. Poison, drugs, sedatives, whatever was coursing through his veins. He hadn't long to leave if he nourished the faintest hope of survival.

Staggering from the hall, he somehow marshalled the presence of mind to ensure both paths were clear of foes before fumbling his way back down the hall he'd originally emerged from. The wild gyrations of his newly rubber legs pulled the carpet to and fro as he shuffled errantly to the edge of the stairs. The corner of Xerdes' vision darkened. His mind reeled as he gawked in mute horror at a staircase that had become an impassable chasm.

He pressed on and found his legs incapable of supporting his weight, tumbling headlong from step to step, hearing bones crack, and feeling muscles shred as he cartwheeled into seeming oblivion. And then he stopped. Gravity had shown mercy, and he found he was still capable of movement... such as it was.

He could no longer stand erect, his knapsack hanging limply at his side as he started down the sprawling corridor leading to the front door. He'd never circumnavigate the cellar. The double doors were his only salvation now.

Throughout the ordeal, Xerdes' throat had imperceptibly tightened so that now his breath came in a shrill wheeze as he barreled ahead, bracing his languid limbs on columns, marble walls, even clinging with wide-eyed desperation to tapestries mounted from the walls to barely remain bipedal.

"INTRUDER!" sounded a throaty voice at his back. Lacking the capacity to turn from his task, Xerdes powered on. He heard footfalls echo in the distance.

Did they echo?

Was that the reverberation of his own skull? His ears pulsated. His vision dimmed as he spilled at last into the Great Hall. Somehow still possessing the coherence to avoid the earlier pitfalls that had led him to this living horror, Xerdes suddenly stumbled, collapsing upon the apron of the oaken doorway.

Groping frantically to his feet, with the aid of the sturdy steel doorhandle, he found himself at last erect. He was only dimly aware of the clatter of footsteps closing on his location as he did.

It required every vestige of will to shelve his overpowering fatigue and attempt to exit. Xerdes found his hand almost leaden as he took hold of the handle, and could—to his horror—scarcely summon the strength to pull the door clear of the frame.

He pulled. The door stood stoically and defied his efforts. The footfalls sounded deafeningly near at his back.

Xerdes strained against its bulk again. The door gave slightly and then stood immobile. He could hear boots clattering on exposed marble behind him. There was but one chance to pry it free and flee with his life.

Xerdes poured every ounce of purpose into one final, goliath outpouring of concentrated effort. The door's mammoth corpulence at last jarred loose, parting just enough to permit the thin thief passage. As the footsteps closed, Xerdes tumbled agonizingly out into the blinding light of the courtyard, kicking the door behind him, and—cognizant of his enemies' impending approach—summoned the inexplicable wherewithal to jam the crossbar with one of the stolen silver blades. The Aven steel was more than equal to the task for at least as long as he would need to escape. His arms visibly shook. His knees collapsed in fits. He had to return.

Had to survive.

Had to get that cold sword tip from between his shoulders.

A gauntleted hand fell over his mouth, stopping Xerdes' weakening breath, another hand pinned his elbows behind. The thief straightened in abject panic. Terror seized his slackening body as his near-sightless eyes darted to and fro, fruitlessly attempting to identify his assailant.

He felt the tip of the blade withdraw while firm hands tightened about him. He could scarcely see through the myopic haze, yet as he felt himself slipping from consciousness, and watched the sky begin to wheel and the earth shudder, he thought he spotted a blade. Long. Angular. Broad. Inlaid with symbols.

Runic ones.

A Horrand blade.

Suddenly, a familiar lock of blonde hair cascaded over his shoulder. As all went dark, Xerdes thought he heard a soft, firm voice say,

"No magic mist to save you this time, sneakthief."

The world rolled over white, and he felt himself melt from existence.

Chapter 4
Deals in the Dark

Ashday, 27th of Ántilián, 1856

Even firelight cast coldly upon the countenance of Inspector Coggins. He was lost in thought as his eyes danced upon the decaying, cheesecake-colored flesh of a recently deceased apparent transient splayed like some cannibalistic holiday spread across a chilly stone examination table. The city morgue was a bleak, chasmal eyesore. Entombed beneath the Menuvian guardhouse, while all too few of his fellows availed themselves of the Corpsekeep's expertise, Coggins had frequent occasion to follow up details and to ascertain the facts of a mugging or murder therein. He had cultivated a familiarity with the Corpsekeep that tended to the murdered as a result.

A rarity outside Menuvia, as the Senate had seized further influence, 'progress'—at least, as they defined it—had bubbled to the fore, necessitating the advent of new positions, often from thin air. While others, such as dog wrangler and stone polisher, were fashioned for the transparent convenience of the out-of-work relations of the reigning elite, Coggins had found the Corpsekeep useful more than once and prayed the post would be a permanent one.

"Crushed," Coggins heard the man say in his dispassionate whisperlike way.

"No blade. No arrows. No sign of a bludgeon though he suffered superficial bruises to the face and body..."

"I see no visible sign of anything being crushe—"

"—my sentence was unfinished," the Corpsekeep continued, firmly, but without malice. "The windpipe. His throat."

A gloved hand emerged from beneath the Corpsekeep's billowing brown robe, indicating the violent bruising on the dead man's neck.

"Collapsed. Crushed. As if by a stockade. Perhaps even a hanging though I see no evidence of a rope."

Coggins' eyes peered directly through the corpse.

"He is known to me."

The inspector's hooded companion looked up for a moment but said nothing.

Yet as Coggins parted his lips to elaborate, he heard a familiar bellow at his back and whirled. The familiar sheen of Captain Bevens' skull betrayed the new arrival's identity before even glancing at his face.

"Coggins!" he boomed authoritatively, like a proud lapdog, eager to sound bigger than it is. The Captain pulled beside his subordinate and considered the body before them. "Related in some way to the Thraxton affair?"

"Admittedly no, sir. A continuation of the tavern arson in the Cloventine."

"The drink den that dropped to cinders?" interrupted Bevens with a twitch. "I've inquired after your report for two days. Seemed a case of straightforward negligence."

Coggins gestured to the corpse before them.

"Myron Lark. Noted fence and fixture of the Gylvain underworld. With a reputed affiliation with one Cyrus Welliver. Proprietor of the Cröd's Den, in whose company he was last seen alive."

Coggins had combed the scene the following morning and found no shortage of witnesses to place the two together at the very tavern the night of the crime.

Bevens leered dismissively at the dead man on the slab.

"...and then was borne by nightwraiths to expire in a spot over a block's distance from the site of the fire?" he offered derisively. With an awkward, familial affectation, he then placed a hand on his subordinate's shoulder and proceeded to patronize. "Coggins, you know I value your eye for detail. But you're seasoned enough to know not all details of a case are pertinent. Sometimes a knife on the floor is for buttering bread. That a guttersnipe dies the same day as another is no proof of a grand conspiracy. Lord Thraxton's burglary is our top priority."

Coggins' cold, masklike demeanor remained unmoved. This was not the first time his concerns over curious circumstances had been dismissed by his superior.

As Bevens whirled, secure in the knowledge his patrolman had been sufficiently placated, he threw a dismissive wave.

"I expect your report by midday tomorrow, Inspector."

As he rounded the corridor and disappeared into the darkness beyond, he thought he caught a momentary glance from Coggins, whose algid glare now narrowed in methodical introspection.

His suspicious gaze focused now, exclusively, on him.

"Xerdes..." a low voice muttered, "Xerdes, Xerdes, Xerdes..."

The words thundered against the walls of the thief's skull.

"Would responding get you to stop?"

"No. Just repeating it until it sounds less ridiculous."

"And...?"

"I decided I haven't the time."

The haggard burglar found himself festooned across a well-appointed couch, his limbs draped languidly over each sloping side. The unmistakable crackle of a tended hearth cast weird, sentient shadows in all directions. He found the black velvet shapes sprawled across his venom-ravaged frame were cast by the crime lord Rolf Eghenston, leaning against the fireplace, and two towering lieutenants who, even now, loomed above him with blades drawn. Turned as they were, away from the fire and toward the rousing thief, he found their features wholly obscured.

"You're a man of skill."

"That's one opinion..." Xerdes groaned, as he learned the hard way that he remained incapable of sitting erect.

"Regardless of your present predicament, I mean," returned Eghenston, his smoky timbre seasoned by the faintest Göurnoth accent. "For all you're at my mercy over the triggering of one trap, my review of the mansion found at least seven snares untouched."

Xerdes tried to appreciate the backhanded compliment, but the sandpaper in his throat, the molten lava in his veins, and the cacophony in his skull had other designs.

"I've executed lesser thieves. Albeit with more nefarious intentions than to pinch some pottery," Eghenston said with an off-handed gesture toward the half-open sack of Xerdes' loot now residing at his feet. He was working his way, now, across a floor carpeted in lush carmine. Xerdes had little recourse but to listen. Unsure whether the toxin he'd been injected with was fatal or fleeting, he got used to the view from under Eghenston's thumb. The mysterious interlocutor continued.

"I find myself intrigued instead. And posit a proposal..."

"If this is a job interview, I can think of better venues than my deathbed," Xerdes finished darkly.

Eghenston had now fully traversed the room, which even Xerdes' muddled mind now conceded was one of the cyclopean side-chambers he'd surveyed on the second floor. Lavishly adorned, its vaulted ceiling had become a stygian void yawning in the darkness. He was the very double of the bust he'd spied earlier: a man of at least middle age but no less imposing. Only his sharpest features cut through the inky silhouette. That, and the clear outline of an ivory-hilted dagger at his hip. Its gold intaglios caught the thief's eye immediately, even in his waxened state. He saw a being of unbending steel, grayed, but anything but wizened. His was a stalwart comportment, and if the frosty mane atop his head, and identically hued, impeccably trimmed beard betrayed his many seasons, his considerable height, and economical, oaken build did the opposite. Attired entirely in black, brown, and gray leather, he struck the thief as an undertaker who'd missed his calling.

Xerdes knew now without question he was in some way related to Wulf Eghenston. It was like looking at a living portrait.

Of a man who had been as close as anyone came to Xerdes' father.

And then who had suddenly died.

"I am offering that explicitly," Rolf returned, his tone as cold as a gravestone.

Xerdes felt a piercing pain near his heart. His wince must have registered, for Eghenston immediately added, "Cramping and spasms are normal. You will be quite recovered within a day, young thief. It's a fool who leaves his treasures unguarded..."

He saw his silver-faced host reach into an adjoining pouch at his belt and produce a small vial of a milky substance. "...but a greater fool who plays with poison without an antidote. You were inoculated as you slept."

"You're an odd kind of inquisitor," Xerdes mused, as his eyesight began, for the first time, to fully align. "Giving me what I need before you get what you want."

Eghenston briefly regarded the henchman to his immediate left. Despite being steeped in silhouette, Xerdes could clearly discern he was a man of staggering stature. "The Darkling venom would have stopped your heart before you awakened had I not intervened. My men still have blades trained at your heart. I've bartered your life in exchange for your cooperation. Would you care for a refund?"

"You shouldn't even be giving him an option," he heard the shrouded form to Eghenston's right say. "A life for a life. He owes us two."

Even if he hadn't recognized the female voice, Xerdes would have immediately identified the scent. Like rose petals on hemlock.

Saryss.

"What can I say?" Xerdes jibed. "I share your love of intruders."

Saryss began to lunge forward. Rolf's hand intervened.

"Athros and Dunwyn suffocated in that demon mist!" she shouted and whispered all at once.

Rolf shot her a silent glare. Even largely enveloped in shadow, Xerdes watched her recoil, cowed into reluctant subservience.

"I'll not labor the point, my boy," he said, returning to the matter at hand. "You're a rough-hewn talent. But with time and pressure... let's just say I've made more out of less. Would you care to...?"

Rolf's hand seemed to gesture to an end-table near the immobilized infiltrator's feet. On it, dimly outlined in the distant firelight, was a carafe filled to the brim with a lustrous red liquid.

"No thanks," waved off Xerdes. "...as eager as I am to drink in the same place I was poisoned." Eghenston served himself, all the same.

"Virailles Manor," Eghenston said, seating himself on a rigid-looking chair and pulling it close. His chiseled, ghostlike visage now fully visible to the slowly recuperating thief.

"Nice place," Xerdes said, and he found he could suddenly sit up. "The Osten Family is old. Connected. And more loaded than I plan on getting after we wrap up this little playdate."

"We're cleaning it out," stated Rolf Eghenston, sinking against the high back of his chair, fingers steepled in a perversion of courtly introspection. Xerdes momentarily forgot to breathe.

Virailles Manor was more palace than mansion. It was a sprawling, elephantine estate second only to the high halls of the Senate itself. It had been the seat of government in Menuvia—and all of Vale—before the surrender to the foreign invaders had changed all that.

When the Senate had formed in the aftermath, they made sure to buy a bigger building.

"So you are planning to kill me," Xerdes had by now caught his breath. "By marching me into a death trap."

"The Undervaults of Kara'Zin. . . Kenoth Palace. . . The Ore Depositories of Sensenal. . ."

Xerdes' darkly set eyes visibly widened. Rolf had named places he had—over the last five years—robbed. Eghenston leaned in to better appreciate the wily thief's reaction and added, "Some might describe those as death traps, lad."

Xerdes suppressed his mounting unease and confined himself to ritual sarcasm.

"You know the job. The less you like danger, the more you make its acquaintance."

"And did you find the reward reflective of the risk?" Rolf followed up, almost before his guest had finished.

". . .never matches the brochure if that's what you're asking. But we both know you're not asking."

Rolf was statuesque in the flickering firelight. He moved nary a muscle, even to speak. Xerdes filled the silence with further clarification.

"I got a long way in this racket by not waltzing into an active gang war."

"...then you should also know when ongoing efforts are above the paygrade of a simple picklock."

Xerdes shrugged in silence. Rolf read it as ascent and softened his tone for the continuance.

"Welliver is no longer a concern. He might once have been counted as a rival, connected as he was to key figures in distribution, smuggling, and other... services, in the Gylvain. But the Cloventine has come far. It has outpaced a bawdy barkeep spinning conspiracies from behind a soiled apron. The war—if it ever was one—is over."

As if reading Xerdes' slowly unfogging mind, Rolf's henchmen slowly closed on the prone thief. They must have spied him mentally measuring the distance between the exit and himself. Close as they now were, he could see their features clearer. A goliath stood stoically to his immediate right, hand firmly fastened to the haft of some manner of hatchet secured to his waist. A long briar of unruly chestnut dreadlocks was pulled back from the sides of his skull, tied back into a ponytail with a leather cord. The stern, expressionless visage scrawled his occupation across the sky: hired muscle and not the cheap kind. To his left, on Rolf's opposite side, stood Saryss, whose marble complexion, sculpted physique, and mane of blonde ice the thief recognized even in silhouette. She wasn't much shorter than the golem on the opposite end of the room. Horrand women were built like that.

With a barely perceptible smirk, Xerdes turned back to his host.

"Awful lot of stick for so little carrot."

Rolf at last registered a reaction. He dropped his hands and narrowed his leveled gaze.

"Then we've found it at last, young thief," Rolf said, wanting Xerdes to ask what 'it' was.

Xerdes obliged.

"...'It'?"

The baron of the underworld stood in perfect silence and whirled toward the door. The brisk suddenness took even his lieutenants off-guard.

"...sir?" Saryss whispered after him.

Eghenston snapped once and nodded toward the couch, indicating to the feeble form of Xerdes before walking out into the adjacent hallway. With wordless acknowledgement, Saryss dropped, hooked the convalescing thief's arm over her shoulders, and began to pull him to his feet.

"Brecken!" she spat, and the other hulking guard took his other arm around his neck, propping the recovering thief up as they made swift exit to follow Eghenston into the corridor. He now understood this to be the same long second-floor hallway where he'd previously avoided detection at the hands of Eghenston's hapless house guard. He could feel sensation returning to his feet but let them drag all the same. 'Let the thugs earn their pay,' he silently mused.

'...and if the prisoner they presumed was immobilized by poison should suddenly spring to life and make a hasty exit? What a tragedy that would be.'

At length, the hallway began to round into a semicircle near the back of the estate, coming to a convex point, where a set of bulky metal double-doors stood latched in forbiddance. Yet the doors, bafflingly, bore no keyhole. Just as his curiosity began to crest, he felt a stiff blow to the side of his head, and the two guards whirled around to face the opposite wall. It didn't knock him unconscious, nor was it meant to. Yet in his weakened state, Xerdes could scarcely distinguish anything before his eyes but a moving floor. When he at last returned to cognizance, he found he was already inside the room, the doors inexplicably sealed behind them. Brecken and Saryss had now propped their disoriented prisoner on a back wall, where he struggled to right himself. When he finally pulled his eyes from the floor, they could scarcely process the sight before them.

Sprawled to the ceiling was an orderly vault, with ill-gotten goods piled atop hills of purloined valuables. All regimented, with each denomination of currency stacked in kind from the smallest to the largest. He'd plundered the secret stores of the depravedly wealthy before, of course, but this was different. Bank-like. Austere. A monument to decades of unparalleled planning and unerring execution. If his apprehension hadn't made the point, this stated it precisely: These were professionals.

Xerdes' booming skull had nearly lolled back to consider the floor once again when a leather sack the size of a small dog or a large cat clattered and spilled at his feet. The top barely fastened with a cord, a half-dozen gold Tirions came to rest at the tip of his boots. It was still virtually full.

Xerdes had to collect himself before reacting. "Is this what we've found, Rolf? Gold?"

He looked up to find a canny smile fixing itself to Rolf's marbled features.

"No, lad..." he began. And in a single motion, he dropped another bag of gold, this one the size of an infant, at Xerdes' wavering feet. It made a sound that was pleasant to Xerdes' ear. "What we've found is common ground."

As incentives go, it had a certain understated allure. Like paying a bar tab with molten silver.

"A rich robber? What are you in this for? The rush?"

"Just because one has much does not mean one has enough, lad."

"So I see. And all this for one job?"

"By the Old Gods, no!" Rolf chortled. "We'd bring you on. Crack some mansions. Work up to it. See how you dance with a knife at your throat. Then take this gilded charnel house for all it's worth and skip town entirely."

Xerdes scarcely heard him, locked as he was in a monetary reverie. At length, he at last replied.

"Virailles Manor sounds beautiful this time of year."

The torchlight danced seductively on the few coins that had fallen floorward, casting a grim shadowplay on the walls around the four conspirators. Xerdes might have stopped to admire it if he'd bothered to look up. He must have stared for an interminable duration, for when he tore his eyes away from the gold's firelit gleam at last, Xerdes found his crimelord companion was now eyeing him with wary circumspection. The thief found himself equal parts puzzled and irritated.

"Do your moods come with a floorplan?" Xerdes scoffed in wonderment.

"Merely deciding if I'm comfortable with how quickly you changed your mind."

"In this line, you learn to recognize when you're getting in your own way."

43

Rolf's eyes narrowed for a moment, and then his features gradually softened. Xerdes soon found an arm had been extended in alliance. He took hold of it instinctually.

"Splendid," the big shot purred.

The cage door slammed shut, jarring them from their momentary ceasefire. Saryss and Brecken made to lift the thief once more, preparing to exit the vault. He whirled like a nervous feline before they got there.

"Strange as this might sound, I've gotten along fine all this time without multiple elbows to the head," Xerdes said, anticipating another assault to keep the crimelord's vault mechanism a secret. With that, he tore a long, thin shred of fabric from the edge of his cloak. "Where I come from, we have a fine new invention called a blindfold. It prevents dashing young thieves from receiving two blows to the brain in one evening."

Saryss looked at him like feces on a flowerbed. She snatched the improvised blindfold from her newfound 'ally' and tied it so tight that Xerdes could hear the blood coursing through his own ears. They departed the vault immediately, the door closing with a heavy, curious mechanical sound that was nigh-indescribable, even to a seasoned safe cracker. Untying the blindfold, he could see his new employer and his guard starting down the hallway already. He began to do likewise, in the opposite direction, when he suddenly stopped.

"Oh, just one last thing, before we start up the minstrels..." Xerdes suddenly remembered to ask.

Rolf paused, turning to his departing guest.

"...the 'lesser thieves' you executed. Who were they?"

"Why Mr. Xerdes," Rolf smiled as he turned back down the hallway with perfect nonchalance,

"...they were your predecessors."

Chapter 5
Honor and Thieves

Lórday, 10th of Vilnás, 1856

The weeks that followed were a portrait of illicit efficiency. Clockwork larceny. Job after job. Theft after theft. Petty burglaries became meticulous heists. Xerdes had pulled his weight. Saryss soon revealed they had looked for outside talent largely due to more recent jobs going sideways. This had been an airtight outfit. Such failure was neither acceptable nor tolerated.

One evening, beside the fire—ironically in the very same room where he'd awakened from a poison-induced stupor—she'd suddenly confided that innocent lives had been taken during the botched scores. The Tolwhyte Brewery Job had been bungled to such an extent that an elderly housekeeper had to be silenced. Permanently.

Her chilly facade faltered briefly as she eulogized her former compariots, Athros and Dunwyn, to the man she'd blamed for their deaths.

"They were fine friends. Loyal," she began, without sparing one look for Xerdes as she did so, "But when I remember Athros sinking his blade in... i-into that old woman's che—"

She took a deep drink from a frothy mug at her side. A pregnant pause followed.

"...Dunwyn disposed of the corpse. I never truly forgave them," she finally finished.

Murder was a matter of debate among organized thieves. Independent guttertrash could, and often did, imbibe. But among true craftsmen? Some felt profoundly about its utility or at a minimum, the need for occasional application of force. Others felt it unprofessional and even moralized about the line between burglary and homicide.

Xerdes, while not averse to lethal combat when no other choice presented itself, fell decidedly in the latter camp. If he had performed his job properly, his presence could be explained away with a draft from an open window, and no one in the vicinity would be aware they'd been hit until hours or even days after the fact. Theft was a fine art, and Xerdes was an adept, arcing toward master.

"You can put a muzzle on a dog, but he'll never forget how to bite," he commiserated, turning his cross-legged frame to the firelight and expecting at any moment an angry reprisal from the fiery-blooded Horrand woman. It never came.

The icy barrier between them had shattered several jobs back. Neither seemed to need to acknowledge it. Which was fortunate for them both, as in the previous weeks, Saryss and Xerdes had been tasked with an improbable number of jobs as a tandem. From a bank hit in the capitol city of Tirionus to simple carriage robbery in the peasant village of Romatho, whatever the woman's reservations about working with an outsider, begrudging accedence had given way to unqualified respect.

Professional respect, with an undertone of something more.

Vicday, 11th of Vilnás, 1856

Rain lashed at Xerdes and Saryss as they ducked under a squat bush in the Valen wilderness. The blinding glamour of the thieves' life had brought them to an unnamed backwater in the southernmost edge of Tunwood, a day's ride northeast of Menuvia.

"We can't possibly be getting a large enough cut for a caravan robbery," Xerdes half-whispered, half-yelled as the unremitting barrage of corpulent raindrops thudded heavily against his drawn hood.

Even over the storm, he heard Saryss hiss.

"Rolf is a generous man," she stated mechanically.

Xerdes cracked a wry smile. "Yeah, I know his type. He'd happily give you silver. If he didn't have any bronze."

There was a muted bellow of thunder in the distance. Peering easterly off the main road, all Xerdes could hope now was that Rolf Eghenston's tip had been accurate. As Menuvia's lesser districts suffocated in ever-increasing squalor, the Cloventine nobility had found inventive avenues

for profit, most of which were off-site concerns like shipping—or smuggling, as the case may be—or, in this case, plantations. If the loose lips
of his informers were to be relied upon, a small wagon train from one
such farming estate was bound back to its master. A risky proposition,
requiring the constant employ of convoy guards. Menuvian banks had
once offered such an escort, but repeated hijackings—and rising rates—
had persuaded the patricians to pay for their own alternative. Anything
to avoid being parted from their own bounty overlong. The wealthy
always slept better on mountains of their own gold.

Chiseling of this sort is self-perpetuating, however, and once the
banks were eliminated as money-grubbing middlemen, the nobles were
invariably brandishing a meat cleaver and looking for more fat to trim.
First went the quality of the wagons and then the quality of its drivers,
and finally they even laid off the armed escorts, one guard at a time.
If Eghenston's source was to be believed, the owner of this particular
caravan had no affection for overhead. He preferred to camouflage its
true purpose than advertise the affluence therein with over-many experienced guards. 'If,' thought Xerdes. In the wily thief's experience,
a blade to an informant's throat rarely enhanced his credibility. Even
an ornate, ivory-hilted blade, wielded by a practiced professional like
Rolf Eghenston. Three distinct tongue-clicks from the treeline opposite
jolted the two shivering thieves back to attention. It was their signal. The
oafish Delfin—perched in a treetop vantage—had spied their target.

Saryss gave a knowing glance to her grudging companion, sinking back
to the cover of the flenniac bush[1] they'd chosen for makeshift shelter. It
lay at the foot of an immense, rotted oak, propped precariously up by an
irregular beam beneath it. At the base of the beam was a cord. One firm
pull was all that would be required to cast it across the muddy expanse
that was once a road. A simple snare, but Saryss clung fast to the rope
like a drowning sailor. Which they may soon be if the weather didn't clear.
Even through the torrent, Xerdes could clearly distinguish the melodious

---

[1] The Flenniac bush abounds in Vale and Highcrest. Something between a tree and a
shrub, its wide, broad leaves and nearly hollowed and rootless center make ideal cover
from the elements and the eyes of onlookers.

descant of her Horrand blade being partially unsheathed. Xerdes' eyes narrowed, and he likewise freed his blade from its scabbard.

What seemed little more than a fleeting shadow extended irregularly across the road and abruptly vanished in the deepening downpour. Such was the only evidence Xerdes had even started across. By the time the untrained eye could have even registered the phenomenon, it had disappeared. In the unceasing tempest, he waited, directly opposite his partner and just a few paces ahead.

It didn't take long.

The distant thudding slosh of rain-sopped footfalls and voices of riders were nearly deafening in the deluge.

Then, through sheets of bone-chilling mist, came the indistinct figure of a flatbed wagon, all but unaccompanied, save for its driver. A mere two riders—one afore, one aft—all that might remotely belie its cargo. As they crossed the agreed-upon threshold, Saryss at last pulled the rope. The log came free with a lurch, looming in the air for a fleeting moment before crashing to the sodden earth with a violent concussion of mud and watery debris. The driver blanched as the horsemen came to hurried attention. Drawing their swords, both hastened to the front of the convoy to examine the engineered distraction.

They were unaware of the virtually invisible shadow stealthily wending its way around to their back. Around the rear of the wagon, it emerged, lockpicks gleaming in practiced fingers. The wagon was utterly enclosed, yet so very often, the strongbox resided in the back, facing the following horseman, and this case appeared no different. A shield-shaped lock the size of a fist met his greedy gaze. Lockpicks probed and the seasoned sneak listened closely for an all-but-imperceptible telltale click. He'd cracked worse in less time, but with the heavens heaving their contents, Xerdes found himself wiping away near-buckets of rainwater nearly as frequently as finding a catch. When the lock at last gave, it was almost drowned by a low, rumbling thunder. Chancing one last look around the carriage, he saw the two guards, still considering alternatives to them engaging in manual labor. With an eager grin, Xerdes cast wide the lid of the inlaid strong box.

A wooden void grinned back.

Emptiness. Nothing.

The possibility existed that they'd located the strongbox in the wagon proper to better shield it from the elements, but he was anything but giddy at the prospect of diving in back and discerning for himself.

Xerdes raised his right arm up and around the edge of the wagon so that it was fully visible to Saryss, stationed as she at the opposite end of the road. The sign of crossed fingers it bore being the agreed-upon signal that the original plan had been altered. Momentarily secure in the knowledge that there was at least one other person to back his play, the thief pushed up on the edge of the length of canvas, and with nary a second to spare for his safety, drew himself on to the edge and prepared to pull himself into the flatbed.

When a blade met his throat. The kind that looks the same as every other, but means more than most. Either he'd been set up by his new employer, or someone was on to his action and looking to end it. It didn't take long to learn which.

From the billowing cloth came the man holding the other end of the blade. It was the City Guard uniform that came with him that piqued Xerdes' interest.

"Appears we've one less prowler, boys," the man's mushmouth accent boomed, the two horsemen already pulling alongside him, having been always and evidently aware of Xerdes' presence. "And what, may'ap 'ave you been pullin', friend? The Thraxton job, per'aps? The Darksword caravan killin'? Might be we've found the Nightside Strangler!"

"Get creative," offered Xerdes. "You can make it all of the above."

Guards emerged from the underbrush, their footsteps having been clearly camouflaged by the torrent such that neither he nor Saryss had seen nor heard them. A finer snare he could scarcely have engineered himself.

The horseman on the right, features wholly obscured by pounding volleys of spate, offered his expert analysis. "He's a dead man is what he is. Out here. No Menuvian court to trouble with. Could walk him right past a cliff, an' no questions afterward."

"Looks like 'e information was good. We was bein' foll—"

"Quiet, maggot!" the dull-witted guardsman's apparent superior shouted. But not before he'd given Xerdes an answer to a burning question.

Albeit an immaterial one in his present circumstance. The guardsmen had been tipped off. The only extant question was by whom. That, and how Xerdes could possibly survive.

So occupied by these questions was the hapless thief, not to mention the fumbling, dysgrammatic interrogation of his captors that Xerdes scarcely noticed when first one, and then another, guard gradually disappeared from view. At first, it had been a small smattering of guardsmen. Then, the horseman to his immediate left dismounted his perch backward and in seeming silence, the kill concealed by a bark of thunder.

Saryss had gone to work.

The guardsmen's lieutenant blustered on, unimpeded. She let him. The distraction was invaluable.

"I'll learn soon enough once we get back to The Tomb[2], so we may as well have out with your name now, brigand."

The heavy seemed to want a twin-bill performance. Xerdes fed him more material.

"King Relegant. Sovereign of Tirionus. In case you weren't tipped by my courtly manner." A flash of lightning heralded imminent thunder. With few subordinates remaining, Xerdes knew the curtain would fall on his co-star momentarily.

"You'll excuse me if I don't bow, my lie—"

The thunder was ill timed. It came a half-second too late but was long enough for Xerdes' long-winded conversation partner to catch the beginnings of a death rattle from a bowman formerly standing at his side. The lieutenant came to an abrupt realization.

"To arms, men! We're flanked!" he shouted. Little more than a half-dozen blades answered his summons. That was less than half the original

---

[2] 'The Tomb' is the colloquial name for the Menuvian Western Division Prison. Cradled at the foot of the west wall on the edge of the Gylvain District, with a moat beneath and bracketed by guard towers on 7 sides, it's aptly named for foiling thousands of escape attempts.

force. Saryss had been busy. Xerdes unsheathed his dagger and buried it in the side of a guard at his back in a single, fatal motion. He was just quick enough to dodge a lopping stroke from the man to his immediate left. So close was the slash that it pulled the thief's hood free. He rolled to answer with a merciless stab wound in the man's spine. He screamed and collapsed, sword hanging limply from useless fingers.

Saryss swung her heavy Horrand blade unencumbered now. In a lethal flash, the throats of two guardsmen behind her came unseamed, black blood sputtering to the ruddy earth from gaping neck wounds as they folded in gurgling necrosis.

Xerdes, disadvantaged with a shorter blade, concentrated on evasion and subversion. Razor sharp caltrops spilled into the mud from a bag unfastened at his side as he ran toward the treeline. A pursuing guardsman gave chase, only to shriek in sudden agony and finally tumble in a heap, cradling his shredded feet. Saryss ended his suffering with a vicious downward sword thrust. With three swordsmen left, Xerdes threw caution to the wind and cast his dagger hilt-first at a guard clambering awkwardly from the wagon bed with blade drawn. By the time he raised his stroke, the dagger had embedded itself in his heart, and the man stumbled backward into the unarmed and terrified wagon driver in the front seat. The two disappeared into the grisly mire as all four horses whinnied in dismay.

With the two remaining guards before and behind her, Saryss wielded her blade like a madwoman, slapping away one guard's clumsy stab at her back before whirling to meet the lieutenant's more practiced swipe. Errant lightning illuminated the runic engravings along the length of her Gjörgen Khäl at intervals so that even at this remove, Xerdes could see she was an able two-armed fencer. She pirouetted another ill-intended strike at her shoulder and directed a return blow at the guard's belly. Whether the slash itself or the shock of suddenly holding an armful of his own intestines caused him to slump to the ground in pallid horror was anybody's guess. Before Saryss could recover, she felt cold steel embed itself in her side. The lieutenant of the Guard had not been idle. The force of the blow spun her into the muck, accompanied by arcing blood spray.

"Khränd!" she spat with such force that one needn't wonder whether it signified a Horrand curse or not. The guardsman only smirked from ear to ear and slowly heaved his blade overhead for the finishing blow.

Before an arrow embedded itself in the side of his skull. The look of confusion on his rainswept visage was promptly replaced by the cold vacancy of death. Saryss turned to see Xerdes, crouched and armed with one of the guardsmen's bows.

"We'll never know how much better that could have gone," he began, as he helped Saryss to her feet. Blood coursing from a slash wound at her side and matted mud caked on curls of blonde hair. "…but I can hazard a guess."

In shock from the wound, for once, she didn't bother to bandy words with her tenuous companion. Instead, her voice was uncharacteristically sincere as she responded, "My thanks, Xerdes. Another moment and…"

"…and you'd have given him a second smile. Clumsy, leaving weapons lying around like that."

The lingering look that followed said more than even her most forthright expressions of gratitude. It was no surprise when they found Delfin's hulking corpse slumped in the very same tree he'd called from moments previously. His body was just a few arrows short of a quiver. They hadn't even taken him down when they heard it.

"It wasn't me!" came a tremulous shout at their back. Xerdes spun to face the source and discovered the driver, covered in enough blood to open an abattoir, but otherwise uninjured. Xerdes moved over to him, a casual threat in his gait.

"Retain your fear of fighting, and we'll continue assuming that's the case. Though…" the thief's hand fell to the hilt at his hip for effect. The driver had no way of knowing it was empty at that distance. "…some helpful conversation would make a stronger case for your innocence."

"They kept me out of it! I's only the driver! Not even my usual wagon or 'orses, sir!"

"Sworn to silence then with leaves lodged in your ears?" Xerdes called back incredulously. "Tough to tell, being born yesterday."

"Don't mean they were s-successful, sir!" the driver stammered in continuance, "I over'eard just the one name! A night or so previous, when they was samplin' the cargo. Seven bottles worth."

"Seven bottles will buy at least a half-truth. What name?"

The driver shot a glance to Saryss, grimacing beside him with sword still drawn and answered.

"Welliver. C-Cy... Welliver."

The two thieves shared an ominous glance. The game had changed.

Thunder rolled in unbidden reply.

Trisday, 12th of Vilnás, 1856

"This complicates matters," said Rolf Eghenston, turning from the two thieves and pawing at his ivory-hilted dagger amid the waning candlelight. "If Cy is still in league with the Guard, it moves up our timetable. We can afford no further delay."

Xerdes took a break from bandaging Saryss' side and offered a quizzical reply,

" '...still'?"

Rolf was not persuaded to turn.

"Welliver has ever subsisted on his more... legitimate connections. Smuggling in a city without a seaport would be all but impossible otherwise. Guardsmen. Tax collectors. At least one senator. It's the extent that confounds me. I've made inroads, but..." A deep sigh punctuated the point. "...Gylvain gold still spends."

"Name a time and place when murderers weren't for sale," Xerdes said. "It's the good ones that cost. I'm no knight, and I did them in easy enough. But I never signed on for slitting cop throats. Even dirty ones."

"I take your point, lad," Rolf's tone softened but lost none of its remoteness. "But I assure you: I'd assumed Welliver was a problem of the past. His survival presents far more problems for me than yourself."

"How do you figure he cast a line on your organization?" Xerdes spat back. "I was there the night you decided Welliver's tavern looked better

53

as a campfire! Wouldn't take much to twist Myron's arm. He knew me for years. Good enough sort, as fences go, but ask him to sing, and he'll give you a three-act opera."

Rolf shed his calculated diffidence for cold fury as he at last turned. "You led him here!"

Before the bedraggled thief could craft a cagey reply, he heard a woman's voice at his back. Steady, unbending.

"…just as likely, he learned the three of us had been seen sleeping it off in an alley afterward, sir." She shot Xerdes a glance that could freeze a crematorium even as she covered for him. "There's no shortage of ways it could be."

The crimelord locked eyes with Xerdes for a pregnant moment. He finally continued.

"I've lied to you, lad."

"Don't tell me it was just the once."

"Virailles Manor."

"Was wondering when we'd get around to that."

"We won't," Rolf said steadily. "A precautionary ruse for your benefit."

"…and here I was, thinking we'd go in on matching tunics."

"I'm not in the habit of divulging sensitive information to freshly minted recruits, master thief. Nor, I note, are you given to betraying the full extent of your abilities and experience." Rolf's eyes narrowed, "…even to a newfound employer."

Xerdes fell silent. In the periphery of his vision, he felt Saryss probing his face for unspoken answers. Only Rolf provided them.

"I was ever at odds with my brother, Wulf," the crimelord purred, seating himself comfortably on a nearby chair. "I saw nothing admirable in his attempts to unionize the underworld. Thievery and honor are opposite ends of human endeavor. When, finally, I failed to reason with him, we parted. He, with his… Wulf Pack… haggard conglomeration of castaway thieves that it was… and me, with my… organization. Though I must admit…"

Rolf's gaze cut through Xerdes.

"…recruiting children was an inspired choice."

The thief's brow furrowed. "If you call plucking me from a noble's private prison and blackmailing me into membership a form of recruitment."

Eghenston's fingers steepled and not for the first time in their association.

"It was no loose talk that gave you away, lad. It was your singular abilities. No independent has displayed such talent since the Wulf Pack was..."

"...betrayed. From within," Xerdes finished, absent sarcasm of any kind.

"...and you, the lone survivor."

"Depending on who you ask, the prime suspect as well. But I'm sure you paid extra special attention to that part."

"I kept painstaking watch on my brother, lad," the big shot continued matter of factly, "It was merely a matter of checking my records."

Saryss's mouth gaped as Xerdes finally spoke, "Was this before or after you pumped me full of poison?"

"The when and why are immaterial," Rolf recited. "You're a commodity. An investment. When we began our acquaintance, I gave you a stake in our harvest as well as my own. And a rich harvest it's been indeed. I've put aside a considerable percentage of your take on every job as you well know. A sum you're free to withdraw at any time. However, such relationships would be untenable without the apportioned legwork. And I did mine. At least until now, I hadn't been disappointed. Your past is an irrelevancy, lad. Whether you remained true to Wulf's ideals or sent him to the Old Gods yourself is as dull a query as it is impertinent. What we both have a stake in... is your future."

At this, Rolf poured a glass of a rich amber liquid from an end table at his side and cradled it in both hands. He was a portrait of icy calm.

"If your dance is in the final act," Xerdes started, "let's see the grand finale."

Rolf Eghenston, beshadowed in his chair, took a long drink and after a lingering pause, replied coolly.

"The vaults of the Menuvian Guard."

The words drained the air from the room. Xerdes could only laugh.

"With or without my last will and testament?"

Rolf sank into his chair "And why should that be so absurd?"

"Because I've seen Guard headquarters from the outside. And I'm looking to keep it that way."

"It follows that the only man qualified to penetrate a prison is too skilled to have ever seen the inside of it."

"...and what's the payoff? A prison cot?"

Rolf's eyes seemed to glimmer from the shadows as he began, "Substantially more than you, or I, have ever beheld. Items of such rarity, we could auction them in the street and still triple the value, with a full complement of guardsmen bidding right alongside the street urchins."

"I'd match the price just for a straight answer."

"It's no secret a surfeit of burglaries has swept the patrician quarter. Welliver having gone into business for himself. Foremost among these burglaries was the Thraxton estate. The lord of the manor being an antiquity trader of peerless repute. The identity of the thieves is unimportant. The job was bungled. The Guard turned up in time to foil the works. They did, however, recover Thraxton's latest acquisition."

"...an end to this story?"

"The Pearls of Härdöväl."

Saryss and Xerdes both stood rigid, neither chancing a breath. The thief's sarcasm suddenly seemed unbecoming. Härdöväl was more curse than legend. A snowy ruin, windswept by the flurries of the Göurnoth tundra. Once the pinnacle of Horrand civilization, it was reduced to icy rubble by a nameless horror a century past. Much of its wealth was still unrecovered, among them the three priceless giant gray pearls that were once the centerpiece of the Firth's collection. Everyone knew the story. It was whispered to children in the most frigid watches of winter night.

Saryss, to whom the Horrand legend was understandably more personal, let loose an Ägrigörian curse.

"...you're certain?" Xerdes asked.

"Unambiguously. The men being Welliver's, he... obviously made his move first. I learned of it almost immediately. Hence our recent... antipathy. Last I'd heard, the Guard were still scrubbing what's left of his men out of the stonework. I've watched you closely these long weeks, and you, master thief, are the only safecracker of sufficient skill to cast open the vaults and recover this piece of history."

Xerdes was dumbstruck. In a single evening, he'd lost any illusion of trust he might have momentarily harbored for his 'gracious' host... and been made party to what would be the greatest heist in Valen history. He turned to look at Saryss, still hissing in pain from the sword wound at her side, his hazy memory reaching back to the stone slab they'd left Delfin's body to cool upon in the mansion's basement. No. Never again.

"We clear up one fact, upfront..." he began, and the baron of the underworld rose from his chair to meet him. "After this? I'm cashing out. You hired me for a spell, and I stayed for several."

Rolf Eghenston's eyes were unwavering as he offered his arm in solidarity.

"After this, you may well retire if you wish. Permanently and comfortably even. I'll not downplay the risk. Nor would I suspect you'd believe it even if I had. But your remuneration is more than material wealth. Of which you already have much if and when you choose to redeem it. Tavern songs will echo from the Port of Ridia to the peaks of Highcrest about this caper. How many heists come replete with the promise of such infamy?" Eghenston completed, his eyes cast wide.

"I'll settle for the payoff."

A dread chill washed over the young thief at that moment. He felt an inescapable sensation of preordained disaster he was powerless to prevent yet honor-bound to ignore. Shutting out the deafening doom throbbing in his ears, Xerdes took firm grasp of Rolf's forearm.

"When do we start?"

Chapter 6
The Death Spire

Trisday, 12th of Vilnás, 1856

The gears in Lieutenant Coggins's metronomic mind turned furiously. Before him lay a field of blood and bodies. It was all the more alarming since the bodies belonged to a dozen or more of his fellow guardsmen, each one with weapons drawn. Each one had been butchered with ruthless efficiency. A wagon lay abandoned at the roadside's edge, its driver thus far uncooperative, a massive log barring the path forward, with a winding line of pilgrims waiting for the policemen to conduct their business, backed up for more than a mile behind. What the guardsmen were doing here, he'd been unable to ascertain, and ever since shutting down his prior queries into the Cröd's Den arson, Captain Bevens had become a block of granite in a uniform.

Coggins bent before the body of one such soldier, a deep blade wound carving his neck from ear to ear, his dark blue uniform brown with dried blood. The bodies had been here nearly a day. The acrid scent of human decay would have overpowered a less experienced investigator. But Coggins was icy and sedate as he peeled back the edges of the guardsman's gory doublet, carefully examining the untouched chainmail beneath. Turning his analytic eyes downward to the decedent's belt, he identified a small purse pregnant with wealth lying half-open on the Earth. Coggins examined it with inscrutable suspicion.

"Have you found something, sir?"

Coggins was steady and circumspect, turning the change in his bony digits. He didn't even pause the count before replying, "40 pieces."

"...pardon, Inspector?"

"Another in possession of 40 Tirions exactly. The third such purse I've observed."

Coggins rose in deep thought. The recruit examined his pallid, aquiline features for emotion or meaning. He found a fortress of crystal instead.

"Sir. . .?" he at last inquired, abandoning the attempt.

"True or false, Friedrich: Guardsmen are paid in alternating weeks."

"T-true."

"True or false: The western guard are paid the first week of each month. The eastern the second."

"I. . . I'm of the Eastern g-guard, s—"

"True or false," Coggins repeated coolly.

"True again, sir."

"Do you recognize these guardsmen, recruit?"

The young man's face blanched. He leaned in, knees quavering, and regarded the corpse.

"I. . . I've not recognized any of these men so far, sir. B-but. . ." he seemed to be suppressing a vomitous reflex, ". . .they've spoiled some in the s-sun, sir. I couldn't say for—"

"Nonsense, Friedrich," Coggins said and spun to face his neophyte companion. "You wouldn't recognize these men. The west and east only commune for the fall feasts. You are less than two months on the job, and we are only now entering spring."

"I suppose that could. . ."

"These men were of the western division. I recall a few faces." He pointed to a slightly bloated mass of blood and mangled muscle below them. "Seld here is normally stationed to night watch on the Western Wall. He should have been paid the first week of the month. Yet here he is two weeks later with a full purse. And in the exact denominations as his deceased compatriots. All of whom, while murdered, are otherwise mysteriously unmolested."

Friedrich had heard the stories of Coggins' photographic memory for faces. He listened in awe and bewilderment.

". . .nor are night watchmen valued for their frugality in a district with more taverns and gambling halls than bathhouses," continued Coggins before stopping in place and at last leveling an unbending gaze directly in the eye of his companion.

"These men were paid. But not by the Menuvian Guard."

The young recruit found himself unable to break the stare. His buckling legs began to do it for him.

"...but you knew that already, didn't you?" Coggins finished with a sibilant whisper.

"I... I..." Friedrich croaked, suppressing the beginnings of a bowel movement. "I've heard things, sir. Extra jobs. More pay for side work. G... getting paid every week instead of just every other..."

Coggins eased up on the boy. Placing a firm, spindly hand on his shoulder, he passed him in silence, all but certain he spoke the truth.

"The dead men were the wagon's escort. But they were not hired by any bank."

"B-but it's written right on the side of the wagon."

"No, child," Coggins said and turned, pointing a skeletal finger at the brand name pasted on the side. "Because Fellowes, Marsland, and Co. does not exist."

"Then this was a..." the boy equivocated at length before his thought was finished by Coggins.

"A snare. Set by criminal transgressors. For purposes of ridding themselves of competition. That appears to have failed. At a price of two dozen dead guardsmen."

Coggins dipped to examine a man skewered through the skull by an arrow.

"If you removed the uniforms, Friedrich... what would this look like to you?" he asked, as if taking the boy by the bridle and leading him to the natural conclusion.

It worked.

"...a... turf war?" he said in a voice the size of a pebble.

Coggins looked up at his subordinate, eyes very nearly betraying an uncharacteristic twinkle. "You have it exact. A battle between rival factions, likely even opposing territories. Each based out of Menuvia. To put a finer point on it..." Coggins pulled the arrow free of the captain's corpse with a sudden tug.

"...Gang war."

Friedrich's eyes looked like full moons. "I... b-but why would a gang war break out? Why here? Why in the middle of a forest?"

"The question isn't why a gang war has erupted. We've had more than seven such conflicts in half as many years." Coggins cast the arrow aside and whirled to depart the crime scene with a matter-of-fact flourish.

"...the question is why the City Guard are participating in it."

Fallday, 20th of Vilnás, 1856

The vaults lay becalmed in forbidding blackness. No mere knotwork of boxy cubicle containers or row of lockers would suffice for the most craven and depraved metropolis in the whole Valen nation. For no Menuvian secret stayed hidden by choice. Countless break-ins, untimely evidence removals during trial and even the sudden appearance of the selfsame evidence at lesser facilities persuaded the authorities to take drastic action. And so, for almost a century, the vaults stood suspended around a cylindrical centrifuge forged of unbending iron and merciless stone, soaring dizzyingly skyward for dozens of levels. Each floor had its appointed drawbridge. Each operated via lever from the opposite side. Two men were required to obtain entry, and two were required to depart the central obelisk. With no railing across the expanse, the merest miscalculation could lead to a headlong plummet to the cold, unbending stone below. Welliver's housebreakers had learned this lesson with grim finality, their viscera now caked to the cobblestones. The inviolable edifice the underworld had come to call the Death Spire loomed in hushed malevolence, a colony of sword-wielding sentries buzzing through its honeycomb corridors, calling mute challenge from the darkness.

A shadow sprawled in answer to the silent summons. It was a nigh imperceptible thing, little more than a puddle of penumbra slithering across stone and brick. To an idle observer, it was little more than a trick of the light. A lone guard, no less vigilant than any other, passed it obliviously in the night. But a strange thing happened as his torch sputtered in the cavernous gloom. The darksome anomaly moved with

it. Slowly. Silently. Until at length, the guard came to a forked corridor and paused to routinely peer into its inky depths. When suddenly, a single gloved hand emerged from the shadowy nebula at his back, and with practiced speed, unfastened an object from his belt, and soundlessly drew it back into the obsidian shroud behind him in one expert, fluid motion.

The atramentous mass then drew back from the hapless guardsman, winding its way back across the expanse of stonework. The lofty interior was lit only by periodic shafts of moonlight through tall, impossibly thin windows carved in the outside wall, and the occasional torch was brandished by one of the many wary night watchmen tirelessly patrolling the impermeable fortress. Like a black breeze, the formless shade swept up a spiral stair, traversing three levels before reaching a latched door. The stalwart lock fastened at its midpoint at least as formidable an obstacle as the firm, stocky steel of the portal itself. The ebon shade seemed to suddenly melt against the soldered surface for a moment, and in scarcely enough time to draw a breath, a high click reverberated through the cimmerian stairwell, and it was pulled slowly clear of its frame. The shadow spilled through the crack in the doorway like a wisp of stygian vapor, pouring into the sparsely lit gatehouse beyond. On one side, the drawn gate leading to the third floor of the central vault stood erect, forbidding entry to its innermost treasures.

The strange shadow wavered for a moment, and then, in pensive appraisal, it settled and waited.

When an even stranger thing happened.

From the distant corner of the guardhouse, against a cold concrete wall, a second pool of shadow deepened, stretched, and finally swept across the floor to meet the other before it. Then, below a single, crackling brazier dangling from the ceiling, the formless mass became a lithe, hooded human form with a solitary tress of pale blonde spilling lazily from the side. Saryss extended her arm in supplication. The same weird gloved hand extended across the darkness and placed an odd, angular key in the woman's palm. The blackness behind the arm peeled back and became her partner, Xerdes, his sharp features casting angular shadows beneath the brazier's irregular illumination.

"We rehearsed this enough to sell tickets and you forget the encore?" Xerdes jibed with a whisper.

Her blue eyes paled as she realized her error and narrowed as she realized the insult. Reaching for the pack slung over her shoulder, she all but threw it at him. It was heavy enough to make her point.

"If I don't kill the director," returned Saryss.

Xerdes parted the mouth of the sack and inspected its beshadowed contents with a nod. "At least you remembered to bring our three friends."

Saryss pulled away from the lambent light of the brazier and considered a steel contraption with a massive metal wheel mounted in its center that looked like it had been salvaged from the wreck of a pirate ship. She wrapped a glove seductively around it and added playfully, "I guess that makes three in a row for you."

The plan had been long-set, repeated, and rerepeated with incessant protraction. As the exact location of the compartment that held the pearls remained unknown, the partners in thievery would move up the monolith level by level, Xerdes' unparalleled lockpicking prowess allowing them to probe the contents of each in kind with Saryss providing assistance should the law of averages foul the enterprise. She had largely recovered from her injurious rendezvous with the Menuvian Guard in the intervening week, but Xerdes saw how she still winced when she turned the wrong way to leave the room.

He'd found himself watching her turn and walk away more and more often.

The Horrand woman was strong yet far from masculine. Her alabaster complexion and dizzying curves forbade that outright. She was steely. Controlled. Trained. Better still, she could sustain a thought long enough to turn a phrase, however often in reprisal. In another era, she might have made a fine warmaiden of Göurnoth. She was a long walk from the feckless drunks and half-crazed criminals a man in his trade was forced to break bread with. With Saryss, he'd happily bake it himself. He didn't hate the way she looked at him either. But business beckoned, and he'd have all the time in the world to mess it all up once he collected his cut and retired.

Then there was the more pressing matter of surviving the attempt.

Xerdes stepped to the edge of the drawbridge that led to the central spire. A window conveniently couched to its left already showed they were well above the unforgiving earth. A hazy particle mist kicked up by decades of dust and atmosphere already obscured the distant floor from view. Across the chasm, the locked portal to the central vault's first floor taunted them from safety with little more than a stone lip to catch the descending drawbridge should Saryss pull the lever to engage it. It was too far a leap for any man without wings, and the Aviári weren't renting those out at the moment.

Xerdes would not be taking the drawbridge. Loud, lumbering, and cumbersome, the experienced infiltrators had already surmised that to engage the mechanism, particularly in the midnight stillness, would alert every guard from bottom to belfry.

The canny thief unslung the bow from his back and with seemingly inborn expertise, began to string it. Saryss curled her lip at the weapon, herself partial to the personal touch only a broadsword beheading provides. But Xerdes did not intend to commit murder with it nor fire it at anyone with a pulse. He nocked an odd-looking arrow. More pipe than projectile, it was reinforced fore and aft with gilded steel. From a stalwart ring at its rear, attached with a stout sailor's knot, wound a stocky rope. Wordlessly, he drew the bow back, the drawstring groaning against the grain of the wood as Saryss dubiously supervised. Propping one leg on the low edge of the open window, he loosed it. The sound of an arrowhead burying itself in a hard surface greeted his ears almost immediately.

A hard, wooden surface. For above the doorway, across the deadly breach, were a series of wooden crossbeams used to reinforce the floor on the vault level above. Only the very ends were visible amongst the masonry on the wall as they exposed fewer than three inches of wood in each direction.

The thief's arrow protruded from the exact center of the innermost beam.

While Saryss gawked at his marksmanship, Xerdes wasted no time on self-exaltation, instead affixing the other end of the rope to the very same anchor set in a deep recess in the floor that affixed the goliath chains that pull the drawbridge. Pulling himself on to the window's edge, he could clearly see the length of sturdy rope that now comprised his makeshift bridge, a deadly plummet yawning four stories below him. For, as yet another unforgiving security measure, the first level of the vault rested not on the ground... but on the fourth story of the citadel itself, making the first four stories of the vault tower itself little more than storage for sundries and supplies.

"Before you dive to your death, I'd remind you this was your contribution to the plan," he heard Saryss whisper at his back. He didn't even look back to return fire. His heart was too busy turning cartwheels in his throat. Xerdes at last swallowed his sheer wall-climbing terror and steeled himself for a trip of ten yards across a cord a cat wouldn't cross if it were attached to a fish cart. He shut it all out and breathed deeply.

A fear of heights was an indulgence for gardeners. A thief's proper purview is the rooftop.

He felt his arms wrap across the rope and the bottom half of his body draw up to lock his ankles around the same. And then, as if bearing intent independent of his own, he found his body had wormed itself halfway across the fatal pitfall head-first. Saryss held fast to the other end of the rope, as if her own upper body strength would be the deciding factor between success or untimely demise rather than the anchor that bored through the pillars that served as the foundations of the very building. Practically unconscious of his advance, it almost came as a start when Xerdes skull collided with the wall. He looked down, but not too deeply. The lip of concrete before the doorframe beckoned below. He let his legs unfurl and at last let go of the rope, and despite the adrenaline coursing through his body, he somehow landed crouched like a feline upon the precipice. Looking back across the divide, he saw Saryss merely shaking her head in incredulous approval. He allowed himself the indulgence of tipping his hood in her direction and spun back toward the door, already untying the lockpick kit from his harness. A lock the size of his skull embedded in the center of the door taunted from the shadows. He taunted back with a barely hidden smile.

Sometimes, in honesty, many times, he impressed even himself with his expeditious advance. This lock was more stubborn, and given what the city of Menuvia had paid, it probably should be, but when he felt the tumbler give and the picks begin to turn, even decades into his chosen vocation... the sound of a vault door moving inward still made his heart break into a gallop.

The prodigious door heaved inward reluctantly like a languid reptile emerging from a boiling mire. Torchlight glistened beyond the barrier, for the guards surveyed these vaults at regular intervals. His own intrusion had been perfectly timed to give him 10–15 uninterrupted minutes of solitude with the collective purloined wealth of the most affluent metropolis in all of Vale.

It didn't disappoint.

Gold. From the floor to the towering ceiling. No gems, jewels, or even coins of the realm. Lustrous caramel ingots, stacked in bullion bars, piled in nuggets. The internal organs of the unassailable Death Spire splayed before his eyes. It was a veritable sea of specie, a vault of breathtaking scope and incomprehensible value. Xerdes had to steady himself at the sight.

Yet it was all a glorified preamble to what lay at the center of the auriferous semicircle.

There was a pedestal, no taller than Xerdes' hip, of a flowing Aven design. It was bathed in an eerie blue light that seemed to emanate from nowhere with three gray pearls that appeared purged of all imperfections, their surfaces seeming to swirl with an ivory ether.

All three pearls were hovering and turning in mid-air.

Xerdes' features twisted into a briar of revulsion.

"Magic," he hissed audibly. "It had to be magic."

There was nothing for it. In Xerdes' limited experience with the unnatural and profane, the only approach remotely conducive to success was to weather the phenomenon face first to learn its limits. The thief boldly traversed the room, fixing his pick kit to his belt as he went and preparing for the worst.

It didn't disappoint either.

No sooner had the unearthly azure aurora touched the top of his upper arm than he was hit with a blow like a runaway stagecoach. That it was invisible didn't soften the impact. Xerdes was thrown clear of the mountain of plunder, and his back smacked the far wall with a nauseating crunch. He lay folded in a human laundry pile for far longer than he would later admit.

Groaning in misery, when he returned to his feet, he brought a better understanding, and a crushing headache, in tow. He'd never passed from consciousness, but he'd wasted precious moments in mortal agony. Fewer than five minutes now remained. Most ominously of all, the weird blue light had transferred to his body, still clinging faintly to his flesh. It was a simple repulsor hex, the kind cages were enchanted with in a warlord's mansion. Usually with two-legged company inside. The kind whose last cage was a crib. The spell could focus inward, as with a prison, or outward, such as the one he'd just experienced. In truth, it was little more than a nexus of kinetic energy—focused, perpetual momentum.

One that could only be undone by yet more momentum.

Unspooling the bow from over his shoulder, he'd fired another cord into the wood crossbeam on the ceiling before bothering to draw a breath. It sank deep. He pulled the rope hard to make sure. Aware he had mere minutes to accomplish his goal, he took firm hold of the rope and began to expertly ascend a pile of gold ingots stacked wantonly against the wall. When he reached the apex, Xerdes unfurled the large loot bag from his back, holding it partly open with one hand, and clinging to the rope desperately with the other. He had just enough space to take a running leap—not that he made sure before he did it. Soaring in a circular arc that carried him directly into the path of the pearls hovering phantasmically in the air, he held the mouth of his bag wide, slammed shut his eyelids, and braced for catastrophic impact.

It appeared as advertised, violent and teeth shattering, and it sent a shockwave that rocked the foundations of the Death Spire and echoed soundlessly throughout. It rattled the room so turbulently that the arrow and rope came unfastened from the ceiling, but that mattered little at this point. The thief had flown true, his mass had carried fully through the phenomenon, and the weird blue illumination had dissipated like a cloud as he passed through it. By the time he saw the wall of precious metals racing to meet him, he had no choice but to release his grip, tuck his head into his body, and roll free to the floor.

Xerdes whirled like an acrobat, cartwheeling hand over head repeatedly, until he at last planted his feet and halted himself with uncanny agility mere inches from an embankment of bullion that would have easily cracked his skull like a ripe melon.

Panic suddenly seized him. He looked down and didn't see his loot bag anywhere. It had darted from his grasp in the pandemonium. His eyes scoured the room in frantic abandon, darting from loot pile to pedestal.

Finally, he spotted it: a mound of obsidian velvet crumpled lazily in a corner. He dove across the room and peered inside.

Three massive gray pearls peered back, the bizarre argent ether still swirling deep inside.

The Pearls of Härdöval were his.

Hastily, he unloaded the other sack Saryss had given him. Three glass facsimiles of the pearls sprang from its depths. Unlikely to withstand serious scrutiny, but equal to the task of momentary distraction, he lifted one orb at a time into the pale remainder of the odd light and watched them suspend there above their pedestals, strangely revolving about an invisible axis. When all three were in place, Xerdes bolted for the entrance.

With precious seconds to spare before patrolling guards stumbled on his shopping spree, he shot out the door, leaving it unlatched behind and stepped out onto the stone ledge at its back. He looked up, expecting to see his makeshift rope bridge above.

Instead, he saw the Death Spire looming above and across the adjacent void... his arrow, rope still attached, dangling limply from the window on the opposite side. The hex's concussion having pulled it free from the other side. With the other arrow already shattered by the blast, the thief stood helplessly on the verge of his own imminent death.

Xerdes was trapped on the other side.

"There's nothing for it! I'll have to lower the gate!" Saryss whisper-shouted.

Sliding the strange, angular key into a recess beside the drawbridge wheel, she heard Xerdes' voice call back.

"If you don't do it, I'll get somebody who will!"

She gave the wheel a violent yank to keep from throwing it at him. With a wooden groan and a metallic squeal, the drawbridge began to shudder its way across the atramentous void. The bellow resounded throughout the cavernous citadel like a rockslide in a monastery. If they hadn't dropped a stitch with the guardsmen yet, they'd be sure to pick it up now. Saryss stopped and listened, daring not engage a single muscle. The building held its breath.

Then came the clatter of boots on brick. The rustling of chainmail and leather. The shriek of springsteel loosed from a dozen scabbards. Distant. Reverberant. But growing louder.

By the time Xerdes scampered across the bridge, guards were already testing their boots against the guardhouse door.

"Another foolproof plan," Saryss gasped, feeling for the haft of her sword.

"Some things I play smooth. Others I play like a limestone quarry."

"…and this time you fell in the quarry."

Another vicious blow to the door. The hinges groaned for mercy while the top corner began bending inward.

"Then grab a pickaxe because so did you."

Xerdes nocked a regular broadhead arrow and bent the drawstring back, unerring aim trained at the doorway, anticipatory of the inevitable attack. The impacts came closer together now, focused and ferocious. But just before the door bent over double and dealt death to the both of them, the sound of sword clashes came ringing from the other side of the stairs. Whoever had been battering their way in, someone had returned the favor. It was the only way out for either of them regardless. So the thieves stood stalwart, weapons drawn, and prepared for fresh doom. The din intensified. Screams rent the night, wavered, and were extinguished.

The door shuddered for a moment and then stumbled inward like a one-legged drunk.

Beyond the verge stood row after row of swarthy swordsmen, dusky haired, filthy, and evidently effective. For a small army of guardsmen lay slain at their feet.

"I'd let that bowstring have a rest were I in your position," a flinty voice bellowed at their back. The men parted shoulder and from far at their back emerged a mountain of a man. One Xerdes hazily realized he'd seen before.

Bald. Sharp featured. With dark eyes and a broad mustache spilling out from beneath a pointed nose.

"Cyrus Welliver," he purred with a smug nod. "No charge for the rescue."

Chapter 7
A Thief's Retirement
(and Other Fables)

Fallday, 20th of Vilnás, 1856

"I won't ask how you've outsmarted yourself with whatever arrangement you struck with him. I won't ask for a larger cut. Reasonable sort that I am, I won't even ask why I was rescued by a man who had your own muscle murdered a week ago," Xerdes said, his eyes unflaggingly locked, across the table, upon those of Rolf Eghenston.

"All I need is my money and a working door."

Rolf seemed riveted to his chair, walled behind a fortress of chilly artifice.

"Open bloodletting, lad..." he started, with stately calm, "is the enemy of commerce. Even of the criminal kind."

"I'll pin a note to the pile of bodies he left in the vault," Xerdes retorted, with a less than subtle turn to the man to Rolf's immediate left. The rival crimelord Cy Welliver loomed there, endlessly amused by the exchange, having not yet troubled to explain his appearance.

"It was always unsustainable, this sectarian struggle," Rolf began. "A city of this size, with so many uniforms in abundance, requires at least occasional cooperation. As you no doubt learned from your recent predicament in the wagon job, the enlistment of agents of the law in... skirting same... is his specialty."

"Seems handy at slitting their throats as well."

"...I hear you're a hand at that yourself," Welliver rumbled from across the desk. His face was festooned with morbid delight at the apparent disunity.

The thief returned his stare. Xerdes saw a cesspool behind charcoal eye sockets.

"You're a yegg of unique talent. That much is obvious," purred Welliver. "I'd thrown half my men at that bloody tower, and do you know what I got…?"

"I know what they got," Xerdes interjected. "A pine tunic and a six-foot drop."

Amusement became bemusement, and for a fleeting moment, the crimelord's carefully cultivated mask of indifference split down the middle. Welliver abruptly corrected, dragging his most practiced smile across his face, leaned in close over Eghenston's side, and added, "Add a few stories to the plummet, and you're in the neighborhood. Cracking a vault isn't the beginning or end of things, Xerdes. I have an entire operation to consider."

With that, Welliver turned to Rolf, extending a hand.

"I'll collect my take now," the rival crimelord said with a grin.

To Xerdes' horror, Rolf parted the mouth of the black loot bag and withdrew one of the Pearls of Härdöval.

"For a job ably executed," he flattered and dropped the gray orb in Welliver's open fist. The ethereal essence at its heart seemed to dull and darken as he did. Welliver wrapped it in a length of cheesecloth and cradling it under one arm, began to stroll blithely from the room.

"Pleasure working with you again, Eghenston," he said with a mocking salute.

Before starting for the door, Cy suddenly paused, standing almost directly at Xerdes' side.

"Always welcome at my tavern, Master Thief. We always keep the home fires lit."

He stepped toward the doorframe and stopped, seeming to consider whether or not to utter the remark to come. He decided he didn't need to consider.

"…you might ask your fence friend. If you find yourself at a séance."

Welliver departed with a wave. Xerdes seethed in silence, visions gliding through his livid mind, of how gleefully Welliver must have watched him twist in the wind, secure as he was in the knowledge of his every activity. Having strangled some from Myron Lark's dying throat and bought the rest from Rolf Eghenston himself. He'd been a rat in a maze from the gambit's beginning.

"...what luck, that there are two other priceless artifacts for you to give away to your mortal enemies," mocked Xerdes.

"Have you any conception of the considerations incumbent on my position? The palms thirsty for grease? The sheer resources required for the perpetual deferment of justice? Did you ever wonder why everyone's gold goes in the pot? Including mine?" Rolf said, wanting him to ask why.

This time, Xerdes didn't.

"Cash me out. Then point the way out of this conversation."

"This is not a bank, boy. Your capital—and mine—has already been committed. To the furtherance of other enterprises."

Xerdes shook his head, "Sounds to me like it's been committed to the furtherance of your furtherance."

"...such endeavors having been completed, you will at that point be paid out. In full."

"...dangerous words to throw at a man who nearly plummeted to his death for the 'furtherance of those endeavors.'"

"Is this all you've come to discuss, lad? Crass monetary concerns?"

"I didn't come here for the idle conversation."

"...yet still received my full assurance of remuneration after I've realized the full potential of our mutual investment."

"I didn't come here for a promissory note either. Where I come from, we sometimes work for pay."

"And you have."

"Then I'll be collecting my third of the take now."

Rolf stared on stoically. He began to sink back into a chair with enough pillows to smother a bear. Xerdes extended his hand expectantly. Unlike Welliver, no melon-sized pearl appeared.

"It has been committed to the furtherance of other enterprises."

This time, the jibes, the patter, and the witty rejoinders fell mute. Xerdes stared directly through Rolf Eghenston. Something less stared back. A labored silence fell like a boulder, splitting the air between them. It was a silence that filled volumes and with florid prose. Xerdes' gaze peered past the imposing archon of crime to the aging mountebank weaving schemes behind a mahogany desk.

Reality sank in like a dagger between his shoulder blades: The time for words was past.

Xerdes drew his hood, wheeled, and withdrew from the office without a word, leaving the conniving crimelord alone with his wealth in a room cavernous with questions. One query Rolf needn't speculate the answer to: He felt certain his hired thief would not return.

In this, Rolf was mortally mistaken.

***

Coggins was a lighthouse of solemnity in a sea of chaos. All around the dispassionate detective, uniformed guardsmen blathered and barked orders, examining every available inch of a vault empty of answers yet still containing at least a portion of its original wealth. The burglars had bagged no small amount of monetary wealth in the aftermath of their combat with the vault guards, but the sheer volume precluded its complete removal. But the vault was far from Coggins' clockwork mind. The gears grinded onward to the inescapable presumption that this theft—and so many before—was an impossibility without inside help.

The wagon robbery had all but confirmed this fact along with an infinitely more disquieting aside.

Coggins spun from the room, alighted the drawbridge, and wound his way down the stairs, fellow officers all but oblivious to his presence as he did so. At length, he arrived at a double gate at the foot of what was once deemed the Death Spire. It was the only available route the swordsmen responsible for the massacre could have taken.

Bending to the Earth, he examined the frame from top to bottom along with the lock. None but the standard scuffs from regular wear and tear presented themselves, and scratches on the inner steel, telltale signs of a picked lock, were noteworthy by their absence.

A key could not have been procured, for the first guardstations lay beyond the barrier... leaving a lone possibility: An inside man had parted it on their behalf.

A THIEF'S RETIREMENT (AND OTHER FABLES)

Grim facts formulated a hypothesis. For the Death Spire did not employ any urchin off the street to safeguard its illicit reserves.

Cops of the veteran variety were killing—or aiding in the killing—of other cops and accepting pay from a criminal cabal for doing so.

Coggins could no longer consult with Captain Bevens. He was, at a minimum, an obstructionist. At most...?

Coggins carefully considered his next move while the walls of the guardhouse eyed him with wary suspicion.

"I'm through," Xerdes stated flatly. "After tonight, I retire. But... I could use you. For one last job."

Saryss's healthy pallor made her iridescent in the firelit gleam of Xerdes's hovel. Even beneath the billowing cape and cowl, her alluring build was impossible to camouflage. The kind three sizes bigger above and below the waist but inexplicably estranged from feminine frailty. Ashen blue eyes pondered her compatriot's proposal. She said more with nothing than priests say in twelve sermons.

Xerdes filled the silence.

"...if the answer is no," he began, "we never speak of it again and meet as strangers the rest of our lives."

She ruminated for a moment that felt like fifty.

"I'm not sure that's possible at this point, Xerdes."

"Saying no or..."

She stepped from the firelight and pulled deliberately close. Closer than they'd been, even in combat. Even that night, with her knife caressing his throat. Close enough to know unspoken secrets and to tell a few as well.

"We're anything but strangers now."

He looked her over, and his eyes said things his mouth didn't.

"I ask... because in this business, it's hard to make a living when you're honest. And even harder to keep living at all."

"Is that what you are now?" she asked. "Honest?"

"Terminally."

She pulled away, traversing the room and encroaching upon the table. She pulled back and her hood tumbled to her shoulders. A torrent of blonde burst from beneath. Xerdes let himself stare. She leaned back against the table's edge and posed for it. She gave him a look that would stop a stampede. Xerdes found himself wanting to approach the table and did.

"...is that a yes?" he asked, and found that without intending it, he now loomed over her, lurid against the table's edge. Her pallor intensified, and she seemed to strain as he pressed against her. She looked like she could take the strain.

"...convince me," she whispered.

Their bodies collided, their lips touched, and all at once, he was adrift in a sea of rose petals and hemlock.

The night watchman was nearly comatose beyond the gate. He sounded like a waterfall with a cold. Rolf Eghenston fondled the ivory-hilted dagger at his belt and made a mental note to have him buried near one. The crimelord had calculated unerringly. The heist had been an unqualified success, the ill-gotten gains were to be invested in latterly larceny, and all he'd lost in the attempt was a talented freelancer he could now liquidate at his leisure. Little came without sacrifice, and while his safecracking skills had proven profitable, going forward, they would have little use in what would soon be a semi-legitimate operation. The funds from the vault job virtually guaranteed it.

Rolf brushed past another faceless guard and moved briskly down the hallway, intent on inspecting his personal vault. The activity demanded absolute seclusion. He'd hire no outsider to tally the final total. None could be trusted, save himself. The simple mechanism on the door having been installed at his fierce insistence, he made quick work of it. Four one-inch latches lay on opposite corners of the hulking double doors. He quickly pulled one latch to the left. From the opposite corner, he pulled one upward. Another slid to the right. The final, he thrust down, so that with dizzying speed, he stood at once, uninterrupted, among a small mountain of his purloined possessions.

A THIEF'S RETIREMENT (AND OTHER FABLES)

Welliver and his men had been able to take only what would fit in a single wooden chest, albeit one the size of a small coffin. He flung the innermost gate aside with rapacious deliberation.

All at once, he stood petrified in place.

Dangling from its bulging circumference was a small, leather cord, from which dangled a folded scrap of paper. He plucked it and read it, steely eyes narrowing in confusion as he did so. The thong was wound through two loops on the front of the trunk that would normally seat a padlock. In no mood to untie them, he reached for his ivory hilted dagger to slice it open...

...and found an empty scabbard in its stead. Somewhere between the front door and the vault itself, it had been plucked from his belt by an invisible assailant. Frantic eyes surveyed the room, finding everything else in place.

All save one.

A leather-bound accounting book, cataloging all his pilfered possessions. Rolf cocked an eyebrow at the discovery, baffled.

Furiously unfastening the cord, guttural pejoratives now spilling from his lips, Rolf at last unspooled the knot and tore the lid from the trunk.

All that lay at its bottom was a black velvet bag—the exact one which formerly housed the remaining Pearl of Härdöval.

Empty.

A dumbstruck expression all but fastened itself to his features. After lingering, tremulous moments frozen in mute disbelief... Rolf again opened the note and revisited its contents:

> *Payment received.*
> *—X*

Lorday, 24th of Vilnás, 1856

The Gylvain was a good district for bad habits. It was the seedy underside of a gleaming city that secretly sweated sin. Even in early spring, the air seemed oppressive and humid with the balmy, radiating heat of a hundred whorehouses and launderettes—one to desecrate and the other to whitewash it away. There was a libidinous symbiosis where a man could gamble his pay, earn it back by doubling down... and rut it away with a strumpet all on the same city block. High on Salward Street, on a rolling hill that sloped into rows of illicit saloons and dice parlors, towered a tenement at whose highest point, beneath a bent and steepled roof, loomed the front window of Xerdes' hovel. He'd no need to relocate. When he'd been on Rolf's payroll, protection was assured, if incompetent. And now that he wasn't? In his experience, when someone wanted to find you, they'd eventually catch up. That didn't mean he was heedless of the risk. For the better part of a week, he'd hopped from safehouse to safehouse, only now deeming it safe enough to sack out at his own. The move would not be permanent.

Xerdes peered down into the bustling degeneracy below. Steam from a hundred rooftops beckoned him to the streets. The hand sliding steadily across his midriff had other ideas. Saryss locked hands across his bare chest. Her porcelain forearm against his ruddy features made for a carnal contrast.

"Is there some reason you haven't spent it?" Saryss inquired. Looking down, Xerdes saw her hand resting on a bulbous money pouch that had hung at the hip of his breeches ever since the night he walked away from Eghenston's organization.

He hadn't spent a solitary Tyrion. It had become a permanent memento—a reminder that even larceny has standards.

"Waiting for the right occasion. And what about you?" he said as he turned to wrap himself around her. Saryss's toned, voluptuous body now nearly fused to his. "Any reason you didn't stay? Rolf probably wouldn't have suspected if you had."

"I've... enjoyed taking my own path."

"I've enjoyed you enjoying."

She curled her lip mockingly at him and pirouetted away, the raven cloak held firmly to her breast, covering everything that mattered.

80

"You should pack," she enjoined. "We should be moving on, perhaps to one of my safehouses this time... and I've put off fencing this mess for long enough."

"What's wrong with mine?" Xerdes shouted at Saryss as she ducked behind a changing screen.

"Nothing," she said with honeyed ridicule. "Some of us simply aren't wooed to sleep as easily by the sound of scurrying vermin."

Retirement was going well for Xerdes. The first few nights, they'd been tempted to tiptoe across the cobblestones for a fix of adventure if not necessarily for riches. They'd occupied themselves with... other pursuits instead. Unfortunately, their fortune was useless until they'd fenced what they actually had. Myron's death put Xerdes out, but he wasn't so heartbroken he hadn't made alternate arrangements.

Sherfy the Knife fenced out of the Gylvain, and while his offers were a far cry from Lark's 'loyalty prices', he'd proven discreet in the past. That was a valuable commodity with half the criminal underworld baying for your blood. Xerdes packed briskly.

After tonight, they could hole up in the Tháin District, gold in hand, and begin retirement in earnest. Suddenly, he paused, unable to alleviate a mounting, malevolent dread welling up in his stomach. He'd known this feeling before. It had served him ably over the years. He'd even felt it the night he...

Xerdes dismissed the unsettling internal augury. Prophecies of doom were for the sedentary, despair for the inactive. Those without agency or action.

'Not for me,' thought Xerdes, lying to himself.

Chapter 8
The High Cost of Low Living

Vicday, 25th of Vilnás, 1856

She hadn't arrived.

The thought screamed through Xerdes' racing mind as he leaped the expanse separating two tavern rooftops. At the agreed-upon location. At the agreed-upon time. Taking the agreed-upon route. Saryss simply hadn't appeared. It was past the point of explicable delay. A full day and the better part of an evening had elapsed.

Had she absconded with his cut and hers?

Had she been Rolf's plant all along?

What kind of crimelord would send the better part of his bounty along with his emissary, and to what end?

As he passed the cross-streets that demarcated the border between the Tháin and Gylvain Districts, he had all but dismissed the theory. There were easier, more efficient methods of eliminating a lapsed operative than sending along an assassin with half your loot along for the ride. And in their more intimate asides, she'd subjected him to much... but never with lethal intention.

Was Saryss an independent then, eyeing the entire take?

Perhaps she was returning the favor for his prior exploits?

The circular thoughts reverberated in Xerdes' skull as he pushed his panting body to greater exertions. Diving over ledges, leaping from chimney to chimney, rolling from rooftop to rooftop, intent on a single destination.

When he at last reached his hovel, he wished he hadn't.

He knew the scene was ominous when the torches of awed onlookers illuminated the spot. At this hour of the night, the Gylvain made an inkwell look like a furnace. Stopping to catch his breath at the edge of a rooftop opposite, he slid down a rusty steam pipe to street level.

Densely packed in a semicircle around his tenement, dazed bystanders murmured in confusion. Pushing his way through the throng of aberrant humanity, the closer he came to the front of the huddle, the more their bewilderment turned to horror. Nothing prepared him for what they congregated around.

Violently shoulder-blocking strangers until at last he spilled out the front of the anxious assemblage, Xerdes stumbled, very nearly cartwheeling to the cobblestones as he was spat out the other side. He followed the onlookers' eyes upward directly to his window.

Just below which, staked to the spot, swayed the butchered body of a woman. Nearly unrecognizable as a formerly living being, the bloodied mats of blonde hair dangling from its shredded skull identified the corpse with grim finality. A pool of black blood sprawled at Xerdes' feet, drops still steadily raining from Saryss's ravaged body.

Xerdes doubled in agony, heedless of the observers collecting around him.

Xerdes had killed her.

Not with a knife, but with stupidity. He'd learned tonight which of the two cuts deeper.

Yet no tears came. No sorrow choked his throat, and no lamentations leapt from his tongue. He knew no Aven prayers nor Horrand blood vows. He felt only white cold fury—the kind that burns to the touch and makes a black pit of the stomach. All that resided there now was unyielding hatred.

Xerdes found at once that his limbs ceased to tremble. He found that his feet had steadied themselves on the path. He did not look up at the corpse again. He didn't need to. It would be blistered into the back of his mind thereafter.

The thing that rose to its feet then was no longer Xerdes, Menuvian outlaw.

It was no longer a man at all.

What emerged was an instrument of inviolate vengeance.

Sweeping past the gaggle of gawking parasites, grim and undeviating, it catapulted into blackest night.

Its blade drawn.

Sherfy the Knife splayed a wide grin at his customer. The latter was incapable of veiling his disgust. Few who watched Sherfy unveil the hole in his face when he unbuttoned his bottom and top teeth had the constitution to suppress a gag reflex.

"Twenny Tyrions an' no 'igher," said the fence.

The shady sort across the counter nodded rapidly, hand pressed to his mouth, merely to move the transaction along and depart the establishment. He half-believed the fence had engineered his dental downfall for precisely this purpose. He was half-right.

Sherfy loosed a small purse, counting out each coin in turn. Bug eyed and emaciated with greased hair pulled back to the border of an impressive piece of forehead, he resembled a reptile perched on a rock, flicking his tongue at gnats. The customer counted his moderate return and escaped to the fresher air at last.

Depositing the goods in an alcove behind his counter, Sherfy the Knife indulged a knowing grin. Business had been better than usual. He'd come into more money than he'd ever seen up close only recently and seemed bound for a further upswing.

The back of Sherfy's shop was a bramble of beams, cobwebs, and curios. The carpentry was cut at odd angles with stovepipes collapsing diagonally into walls. Knick-knacks and miscellany were strewn across every available surface, horizontal and vertical. On any given night, the shadowplay behind the counter was a three-act epic.

Thus, Sherfy never spied the door behind him open and close itself nor the shadow that spilled into the room and melted against the wall beside it thereafter. He never saw the malevolent shapes swirling in the void, lurching toward him from the cloistered blackness.

Sherfy the Knife spun on his back heel complacently, oblivious to the encroaching void. He remained oblivious when a dark shape slashed at his midsection from the darkness and portions of his stomach spilled to the floor.

A womanly shriek sliced the air as Sherfy the Knife clattered to the floorboards, handfuls of his own viscera cradled in his arms. It didn't stop him from drawing a blade from between the floorboards and shouting a curse between mouthfuls of plasma.

"A sword-wielding type like you shouldn't be so quick to anger," the darkness mocked and punted the blade across the room.

An oil lamp lit itself, its dull gleam only providing only enough illumination so that the silhouette of a hooded knifeman could be clearly discerned, looming over the dying fence.

THE HIGH COST OF LOW LIVING

Sherfy winced. Wide. His tooth collection had not proliferated. Even the shadow momentarily recoiled.

"I am not asking what became of the Horrand woman who came to you last night," it began with a whisper that reverberated as if from a hollow skull. "I already know exactly what you did. And why. And who paid you to do it."

The figure leaned in tight, the tip of the dagger pressing into Sherfy's throat.

"Now tell me exactly where he lays his head. . ." Xerdes hissed from the shadows, ". . .and I shall ease you of your life."

Lorday, 3rd of Dogn, 1856

Rolf Eghenston awakened to the knowledge that another storehouse had been incinerated. This time, it came at the cost of twelve barrels of Thyrdán[1]. Twenty-five barrels had been sacrificed to this particular blaze. It was the third such conflagration of the evening alone, and the sun still hadn't made an appearance. Eghenston needn't labor over the identity of the arsonist. He'd all but scrawled it across the sky with plumes of narcotic smoke. Xerdes.

"On the week, that makes twelve separate fires, sir," Brecken reported soberly. "We've also the three missing couriers. We've scoured the south and east side, sir, but—"

"Save your efforts, lad," Eghenston interjected, his voice beleaguered with many sleepless evenings. His studied diction had begun to evaporate along with his temperance. He had replaced them both with booze. As such, he'd gradually reverted to his Göurnoth accent. "We'll not find them unless he puts them on display for us in the square."

---

[1] Thyrdán: A potent stimulant originally ingested by yeomen of the nomadic, wolven Ferás-sûn to stalk prey for longer periods in eons past. Now the mystic root is commodified, powdered into a party favor for Menuvia's ascendant criminal class and the idly affluent.

Not for the first time in recent memory, Rolf found himself knocking back a glass of Bord brandy in the early morning hours. He'd not intended to, but the bottle had other designs.

"Double the guardsmen patrols. Have them hit her old haunts and his," he slurred. "For all the bloody good it'll do."

"Sir…"

Rolf looked up from his latest glass with a start, as if only now noticing he hadn't been alone all morning.

"…there is the matter of their price."

"Pay it," Rolf said, swilling the remainder. Filling another glass, by the time his subordinate next spoke, he'd already started on the sequel.

"They've… they've asked it be doubled, sir. R-recruitment being soft after so many were slaughtered in the vaults, at the wagon job 'n such…" Brecken found his voice trailing off.

The look Rolf shot him told Brecken the move had been wise, if tardy.

Eghenston examined the bottle's bottom providently, searching for solutions in the caramel elixir. He felt he found one.

"Triple it."

He placed the liquor and decanter back on the desk, groomed his doublet fastidiously, and added,

"…and arrange a parlay with Welliver. We've a mutual pest to exterminate."

There would be no meeting.

For at that very moment, a shadow stole from the fourth-floor bedchambers of Cyrus Welliver, who'd slept—in seeming security—nestled high in the attic of a patrician estate in the Cloventine quarter since the night his tavern was reduced to cinders. The Herion family being so often away on business, it was a simple matter to arrange to rent it.

Like a black breeze, the nebulous shape swept across the room, only to abruptly pause near the doorway. The distant thud of formidable footsteps heralded untimely discovery. Like an atramentous fume, the shape glided back the way it came, settling against the windowsill and converging seamlessly with the blackened brickwork.

A goliath darkened the door frame. Pressing inward warily, for he noticed immediately that his door hung slightly ajar. Then, all at once, barreling into the bedchambers came the colossal crimelord, Cyrus Welliver.

Sharp eyes inspecting every corner and coverlet, gradually, Welliver began to relax. Yet one particular item required a more personal inquiry.

Cy was not a man made for elaborate puzzles, false fireplaces, or impermeable vaults. He preferred instead the personal touch of a dagger's blade when possible. His prized possessions rarely lay in repose in an austere safe deposit box... but close at hand. They were defensible at all times by the only man he ever truly trusted: himself.

Reaching beneath the bed, Welliver felt for a wooden box, letting loose a sigh of relief when he found it. Sliding it from beneath the bedframe, he wanted only one last, lingering look at the weird, milky ether that seemed to swirl in the center of the pearl. Though it could bankroll fifty heists of lesser scale, he'd found it difficult to part with the bauble. More difficult still would be pawning it, though he lacked not for the means. He opened the lid and stared deeply.

An empty box stared back.

Eyes shot wide in confusion and infuriation, another object caught the light out of the corner of his eye. Buried blade-first in his headboard, a dagger hilt protruded. It was carved entirely of ivory, ornately wound with golden intaglios. On his bedside table, the ledger book was also curiously missing.

A wordless message.

Menuvian crime could accommodate but one imperator. Rolf had decided it would be him.

Welliver tore the blade from the bedboard.

This affront demanded an answer. As he caressed the knife's edge, Cyrus Welliver was already assembling his reply.

Chapter 9
The Long Moonlight

Creaday, 6th of Dogn, 1856

Xerdes held his breath like a pearl diver and with a slow, smooth slice, eased the purse from the patrician's belt. Compensating for the sudden removal, his other hand already cupped it like the head of a newborn, bearing it away from its former owner without him once possessing the beginnings of a clue. Silently, it slipped into Xerdes' bag. The noble ambled away, unsuspecting of the encounter and all the happier for it. It hadn't taken an hour for the first fire arrows to fly. By midday, the word was out, even as each side sharpened their swords in preparation for the evening. Their nocturnal combat resumed at the stroke of twilight, as inevitably as the sunset itself.

Over a scant three days, bulletins and wanted posters had already applied purple prose to the problem.

The Long Moonlight, they called it. It was a night war without end or aim, one that paused at dawn's first light and resumed each evening as if it had never been postponed.

Xerdes had set Menuvia's two most prominent cartels against each other with craft and cunning, yet even in his bloodiest visions of overdue retribution, he'd failed to reckon with the intensity of an all-encompassing gang war of this magnitude. Even now, the seemingly inconsequential cutpurse who'd engineered their conflict had found himself forced from the streets by the sheer volume of blood that flooded the boulevards and throughways of the Gylvain. He was now relegated to picking pockets for Tyrions at a time in the Cloventine Quarter, for the crimelords tended to avoid fire damage near their own palatial estates. His traditionally nightly nature was momentarily inverted so as to avoid swordfights with the minions of Menuvian crime. He would do anything to avoid touching the bag of blood money that still hung like a limp, severed arm from his waist. He'd remained hopeful that, by biding his time and bleeding the two criminal consortiums of their manpower and moneyed resources, eventually, the leaders of each would be drawn to more direct action. And revealing themselves, they would be made vulnerable for the final stroke.

The opposite had occurred. For what crime lord ever held a knife when he could hire another man to do the slicing?

Xerdes had, quite simply, underestimated their resources. These were no mere opportunists. Rolf Eghenston and Cy Welliver were entrenched. Their rotting roots were buried in the very foundations of Menuvian society. The more murders he witnessed between two lieutenants who met as strangers that very night and died on each other's sword points while warring over a street corner neither lived on, the light leaving their eyes knowing less about each other than when their blades first crossed... the more Xerdes accepted the immensity of his miscalculation. Neither of these moldering oaks could be felled without uprooting half the 'legitimate' institutions in this putrefying metropolis along with them. Even in the short time he'd been in Eghenston's employ, more than once, he'd overheard a senator's name tumble from his scheming lips. At least once, a baron as well.

He shouldn't care whether the streets flowed brown or red, Xerdes told himself, the self-deception seeming less absurd somehow when it wasn't spoken aloud.

Ducking down an unpaved side street and into a nearby tavern, hood eternally drawn to avoid undue attention, Xerdes made a quiet matter of counting out his coins. He emptied the bag out on the table. The coins made all the clatter of feathers on a beach.

Xerdes sank in his chair. The exasperation must have registered on his face because a tavern keeper with a hedge maze of mutton chops on either side of his head gave him the look of a man minding his own business with difficulty. He pulled the hood lower until the tip nearly touched his week-old growth of beard.

The barkeep was not his only observer. For the second day, he'd spied him.

Clad entirely in brown, from his sepia scarf to his auburn breeches, if drabness were inconspicuous, he should have been invisible. Getting his first good look at him by the dim lamplight, Xerdes could see now he was darker-complected and sallow-featured. Well-trimmed tufts of dull brown hair dangled over an impressively sweaty forehead. The haircut said he was either vain and skilled with a scalpel or moneyed. It may have been precisely these attributes which drew Xerdes eye two nights previous. The man had been shadowing him at least as long. Sensing his quarry's eyes on him, the man pulled the tankard up to his chin and sipped deeply. The move was only obvious to a seasoned sneak. The longer Xerdes observed, the more it made him certain this was no amateur.

The two swordsmen that flanked the fellow told the remainder of the story.

He'd not noticed them on prior excursions. It was a canny move to make the follow man more conspicuous than his compatriots and to draw the thief's attention from them, thereby setting him up for a killing stroke he was certain would come soon.

He knew now information wasn't the man's game. These were assassins. The competent kind. Undoubtedly out-of-towners, as a native would have had no need to stalk his steps.

Someone had hired a pro.

He'd allowed the leering man to trail him for days if only to learn what he wanted. Thus far, he'd learned only that hired blades were still subtle as a battering ram. They were stroking their scabbards in a corner booth like perverts too cheap to pay into in a peep show.

Xerdes looked sidewise at them both. A sadistic smirk carved from pure sardonia adorned his features as he beckoned the servant wench hither. She was built like a barge, wide and sturdy, with all the eye-catching bits spilling from a corset that was audibly begging for death.

She floated across the room but promptly sagged at the sight of him, visibly disgusted by his haggard visage.

As the heavies supervised from afar, he bent her ear and whispered unheard instructions. The wench's eyes widened. After serving him a mug of wine, she waddled to the back, vanishing through the back door without a word. Reclining with perfect nonchalance, Xerdes took several lingering drinks from the mug while they watched him do it.

They hadn't spied the thief's sidelong glance as he'd whispered his meaningless message to her. How he noted their interest with a barely suppressed smile.

One by one, they filed from the tavern. Within moments, only the lookout remained, and at length, even he quietly finished his drink, slipped from his seat and stepped into the street. Behind the establishment, the tavern wench was hovering above a wash basin, utterly apoplectic. Soiled uniforms were explicitly forbidden by management. If this spot wasn't scrubbed, she'd be on her third serving job this year alone. She was mortified a customer had noticed before she had.

A shadow from over her shoulder fell over the wine stained dress, and she twisted with a start.

Three men with the aesthetic appeal of petrified manure grinned before her. One was mousey, his doubled-over, shifty-eyed aspect giving the impression he was not at all accustomed to combat. The second was a behemoth with a bastard sword sheathed across his broad back. He beamed oafishly, secure in the knowledge that a spelling contest was not in prospect. The third was a dusky, eagle-eyed rail of a man who appeared uncharacteristically disciplined for a cutthroat.

"A word, marm," began the mousey one's pidgin inquiry. "We'd only know what words the 'ooded fellow frew at ye."

"...an' what concern is that o' yours?" she shouted and stepped fearlessly forward, more offended by someone prying into the matter of her stained skirt than the obvious malevolence they'd broadcast by doing so.

"Oh, but 'taint, marm," the mousey one winked, his dagger coming free as he did so.

"...it's yours."

The shifty one's skull beat his right foot to the ground. The arrowhead lodged in his neck helped it along. The other two whirled and parted, blades drawn, to face their assailant.

Xerdes cursed. The arrow had been intended for the thin one. He heard the telltale song of steel that can only be made by a throwing knife sailing past the ear. Xerdes descended the rooftop, losing his bow in the process. He fiddled for his dagger, dodging three more throwing knives as he went. The final missile, trained at his head, he'd no choice but to bat away with his blade. With a shriek of steel on steel, it tumbled harmlessly to the mud, the already-bleeding slash across his knuckles bearing testament to the fraction of a second he'd had to avoid lethal injury.

The large one waited no longer, diving at the agile thief, his horizontal slash evaded by a timely roll in the mud. Close enough to stab the back of his hamstring upon regaining his footing, the giant bent in agony from the blow. The scream of pain became a light sob as he folded, still nestling his shattered leg.

From twenty feet away, the oaf looked like he meant business. From five feet away, he realized his only business was looking like he meant business from twenty feet away. The sword was as much a hiding place as a weapon. Not like the thin one. He was subtle. Well kempt. His sleek breeches and black brocade overcoat were tailored to perfection. Built lean for the kill with the economy of a forest predator, he had his longish hair pulled back in a tight ponytail like a fencer. Cold practicality and exacting skill bankrolled his arrogance. Xerdes didn't have to cross blades to know he was not the man's equal. The giant's sword would be useless to a man of his stature.

His only hope was flight.

He turned to run. The swordsman anticipated his action, flanking him in a flash and barring his path with a finely polished rapier. Xerdes kicked it from his path, but the fencer was far too well trained, using the momentum to trip his quarry as he darted to leave. Xerdes fell face down in the mud. Visibility already waning in the rapidly approaching twilight, when he rose, he found that he now could see almost nothing.

"Davien Lucard," he heard the assassin all but whisper.

The bewildered expression on Xerdes' face must have asked the question he never said.

"...it is only proper to die with your foe's name on your lips."

"Yeah...?" Xerdes spat mud and pebbles as he chuckled morbidly. "Is it also proper to murder for money?"

Even through a thick layer of mud, the thief saw a furnace ignite in Davien's eyes. Lunging wildly, Xerdes at last had his opening. He blocked with the pommel of his dagger, pinning the rapier's tip to the earth with his left boot. His daggerpoint was pressed to Lucard's throat in a heartbeat, and he almost felt comfortable saying he had the upper-hand. That was when a forearm hit him so hard across the face that he could hear colors. Xerdes corkscrewed in the air and crashed to the mire below in a vicious concussion of soil and horse excrement.

Lucard dislodged his blade and righted himself. But before he could take another step, he sank back abruptly, his face wearing a mangled amalgamation of surprise, horror, and amusement. For lodged in the left side of his breast, just below the shoulder, was Xerdes' dagger, pinning him to the tavern wall in an almost comical fashion. Aware of his enemy's approach, the thief had hurled it with near-faultless marksmanship. After the shock expired, Lucard attempted in vain to free himself but found it so deeply embedded that he lacked both the angle and power to extricate himself from the painful predicament. Xerdes simply sat cross-legged in the muck and regained what remained of his wind.

Davien Lucard would not let the matter rest.

"Even at bay, I have you," he taunted.

"Among all your assassins, only I understand the sentimentality of a warrior's weapon. You will not leave me until you recover it. And we both know the wound is not mortal. Yet if you come close enough to take it, I promise you will choke on my rapier before the sun falls in the sky." The deadening rays of twilight all but blinded Lucard even as he spat the words.

Xerdes rose, caked with mud and equine feculence. He stared long at Lucard, and there was something of a mockery in the engineered silence. Then, the thief turned and began to walk away, his opponent in utter disbelief. He handed him a cockeyed smile and said,

"But I'm no warrior," he sighed. "I'm a thief. And that's my fourth dagger this year."

Quickly washing himself in the basin while the stupefied tavern wench gawked, Xerdes stepped back out into the street, Lucard shouting curses at him all the while. The clashing of blades in the distance could already be heard, echoing ominously in the night. The rival gangs had resumed their struggle. The Long Moonlight fell again on Menuvia.

With but one candle to guide his hand, Kellin Tifius crafted works of larcenous art. Perhaps it was his preternaturally steady hand, his eagle eye for detail, or his ability to improvise minor embellishments in even the most extravagant script that added to the apparent authenticity of his masterly forgeries. Whatever combination of disparate factors had allowed him to ascend to his present status in the Menuvian underworld, Kellin was a man it paid to know.

Xerdes knew him well.

"You're certain of this?" the master forger asked monotonously.

Xerdes leaned over his shoulder, examining the two sheets of blank parchment.

"I didn't ask out of general curiosity."

Kellin adjusted his monocle and furrowed his forehead disapprovingly. A slight head-shake was the most emotion he'd marshalled in years.

"A letter in Welliver's hand... and another in Eghenston's...? To what end?"

"To the end that we exchange coins for the letters. With that, you replenish much-needed supplies, and we keep you in inkwells and monocles for many years to come. So long as I'm walking you through your job."

Kellin shook off the sarcastic remark and turned back to his table. "No offense intended, Xerdes. You know I never ask questions. But..."

"...I know. I know. Suicide."

"Not at all," said the forger. "Only one person dies in a suicide."

Arranging his pens and beginning to fold his parchment, Kellin ran pointy fingers through a mop of graying hair and said, "Of course, it's all for naught anyhow. I need writing samples from both. So unless—"

There was a heavy thud, and a plume of dust made a halo around Kellin's head in the flickering candlelight. Before him lay two leather-bound ledger books. He flipped through them madly. One was in Cyrus Welliver's hand. The other in Rolf Eghenston's.

"I'll be back for them tomorrow," he said.

A morbid plan had darkened his thoughts of late. It was a stratagem too excessive, too overt even for his blackest, most vengeful ruminations. He pushed it away with thoughts of Saryss. Her sculpted body shredded to crimson rivulets. All but her porcelain face, dead eyed and open mouthed but otherwise eerily untouched. It was an inane, violent end purchased with one of Xerdes's plans.

In the aftermath, he'd made no vow to long-exiled gods or sworn no oaths to elemental forces above or below the Earth.

He had only made a tacit covenant that he would never envision another plan of its like again.

And yet, unbidden, it cartwheeled unceasingly through the thief's skull. Until, at last, presented with no prevailing alternative, he relented.

Xerdes rose from the desk, collected his empty coin pouch, and ascended the stairs to street level. Even as he prepared to violate this silent promise, he permitted himself to forge another.

"This time," he swore, "no one gets out alive."

———

Coggins sat alone in the guardhouse study, chin propped on a bony fist, inscrutable steel-gray eyes peering past the nothingness before them. The gears of his mechanical mind turned over the details of the preceding weeks. The study had a restrained, monastic quality. The high, steepled ceiling was churchlike, and tall, thin windows that swung outward to catch the cool spring breeze lent to the contemplative, sacred atmosphere. It was like a library with aspirations to be a cathedral. Suffocating to some, to Coggins it was now the one place he could assemble his thoughts in relative peace. For he required solitude to consider the events as they'd presented themselves.

"Conspiracy."

What he had unwittingly unearthed could be called by no other name. Guardsmen, and their superiors, implicated in underworld heists and attempted assassinations, their crimes mysteriously annulled when they went awry. Evidence had vanished. Bodies had been moved from the morgue or hastily cremated in an apparent coverup.

Yet it was not the particulars of the offenses that occupied his thoughts. That the conspiracy existed was no longer in doubt. Nor were the identities of most of the core conspirators, save a few key names.

The question was what to do about it.

Coggins had risen quickly through the ranks of the Menuvian Guard. Yet even he was still a lowly Inspector, and under the current corrupt regime, any move he made would be reported to the highest echelons of the criminal cabal. To date, he'd yet to learn how high the tower of graft actually soared, but Coggins's cold logic suggested such a conspiracy could only subsist with allowances from the highest-ranking offices of the Guard itself. Perhaps higher still.

Disengaging his chin from his balled fingers, Coggins was about to assemble a list of names when he saw it.

An outstretched shadow, framed obsidian against the moonlight's glow, occupied the open window, saying nothing. Coggins squinted for a moment, convinced long hours of introspection had beguiled his eyes. The shadow remained.

Soon, Coggins' curiosity overcame his confusion.

"What is it you want here?" he said severely. He was unafraid, indeed utterly emotionless. Merely perplexed.

The amorphous, sable shape drew itself further through the window. A high boot, followed by gloved hands, carried the rest of the body through. A hooded face met the Lieutenant's inquiring eyes, half-obscured in the muted illumination of Coggins' table lamp.

"Inspector Coggins," Xerdes said. "it's time we talked."

Chapter 10
Fanning the Flames

Fallday, 7th of Dogn, 1856

Menuvia burned.

Every evening, the nightmare renewed. Every night, bows were drawn, swords were crossed, and strangers met in mortal combat, and trampled between the two was the city itself. Menuvia was overstocked on killers and short on scruples. Xerdes surveyed the carnage from a belltower high above the Eghenston estate. By now, it had erupted into the Cloventine District, and even civilians were giving themselves over to full-scale riots and looting. There was no use denying it.

He'd given birth to a bloodbath.

Shrugging from his perch, he knew he had no other choice. The overseers of the underworld only understood one language, and now he was fluent.

Xerdes had more to say before the Long Moonlight waned.

Whisking his way down the tower stair, the sound of screaming women falling to the debaucherous wiles of unbridled butchers reached his ears... the smell of burning wood and booze and even the unmistakable aroma of immolated flesh tickled his nose. Secure behind the tirelessly patrolled gate stood Eghenston's estate, utterly untouched by the consequences of his own edicts. Xerdes stole a look over his shoulder to ensure he wasn't being watched and pulled himself up and over the outer wall, his latent agility allowing him to circumnavigate the spiked rods at its apex.

Once inside, he bent low to the ground and approached the massive double doors that he already knew opened into the grand hall, the very site of his collapse into unconsciousness, and worse.

Aware of his surroundings, Xerdes unfurled a thin length of parchment, crept low, and slid it under the gap beneath the prodigious doorframe.

Then the vague, flowing shape dissolved into the entropy of the Menuvian night.

Scant minutes later, the same umbral form flowed past the forward guard at Cyrus Welliver's temporary residence, Herion Manor. It paused, plucked an object from its back, and pinned it to the thick arched doorway. An arrow fixed it to the spot.

It was a letter, written in Rolf Eghenston's sumptuous script and precise syntax.

It was also a forgery.

> Welliver—
>
> Our quarrels have yielded only empty coffers, diminished forces, and costly criminal trials we can neither sustain nor afford in the longer term. Aggrieved as you are of me, as I of you, in the interest of our mutual survival, I propose a parlay. While it is entirely possible it will come to naught, I believe to fail to make the attempt will ensure nothing but our continued, mutual depreciation.
>
> By way of peace offering, I shall deliver to you, in person, the Pearl of Härdöval. No further overtures are required on your part. Only an open mind.
>
> We will meet in a neutral location. The long-vacant Night Gallery in the Tháin District. I own half a stake. Included with this letter is your half of the stake in the same property, ensuring the venue is irrefutably impartial.
>
> The offer stands as written, but not indefinitely. To forestall further depredation to our respective syndicates, I must insist on an answer by tomorrow evening. The night of Khäzmära[1]. What you in the west call the Sörnniad. I

---

[1] Khäzmära: The Horrand New Year. Unlike their cousins in the West, who celebrate the dawning of the New Year more traditionally, the barbarian lords of Göurnoth celebrate the razing of dead flesh and renewal by fire. Every hearth burns on Khäzmära, hosting countless stories and songs from previous festivities. It is celebrated with a feast, but not in observance of the New Year, in Vale and Highcrest, where it is known as The 'Sörnniad', after Sorn, the Valen God of Flame.

can think of no more appropriate occasion than the festival of renewal.

You needn't draft a letter. I ask only your presence and your ear, by way of reply,

—R

The forgeries delivered to both barons of gangdom, the hooded shade traversed the garden of the Herion estate, scaled the mansion wall, and receded into scarlet night. A mirthless, scarcely audible mockery trailed in its wake.

Maiday, 8th of Dogn, 1856

The Night Gallery had earned its nomenclature not in the care-free felonry of recent years, or even the gangland holocaust now lapped at its doorstep, but back through the long years of true, inveterate larceny. The lean years under Cerulean occupation had required a rare breed of criminal class. As imposing an empire as Eghenston and Welliver had contrived, they were built upon the bones of a greater depravity. For even in its violent profusion, the two titans of Menuvian crime were but a faint echo of the underseers of old. Each assigned a ward, and each archlord and caretaker of all who abided within it... the very districts of the city had been specifically carved out in consideration of their kingdoms. These parameters remained in place to this very day, in thrall to new masters. The black markets were the underseers' arms, the canals their arteries, and the very military of Menuvia itself, their claws.

The Night Gallery had been their castle.

It was a palace of perfidy and vice. Yet it was a drab, wooden, unassuming structure, not at all dissimilar in appearance to one of the prize-fight venues or low-rent dance halls that dotted the Tháin District. For while the underseers had assumed unspoken administrative control of nearly all aspects of Menuvian society, they had self-imposed strictures that forbade them to flaunt it. When their enforcement of those rules began to erode, so did their empire. That had left the ideal opening for the ascent of a more refined criminal element: the Menuvian Senate.

There could be no more appropriate setting for this meeting of murderous minds.

Suddenly, a single shaft of light cut the crepuscular gallery in half. A rangy shadow emerged from the middle of it and spilled across the sawdust-strewn floorboards. It belonged to the silver-maned mob lord, Rolf Eghenston. Hands linked at his back, his jaw jutted ahead as he entered the inky expanse. Whatever his multifarious difficulties in the preceding week, he was going to some effort to appear the living embodiment of shrewd poise on this occasion. The distillery scent on his breath undid it all.

The other party projected no pretensions of lordly elevation or meticulous calm. Cyrus Welliver all but removed the door from the frame when he barreled through for the meeting. His feet landing like Cröd hooves on the dust-caked woodbeams below. High above their heads lay a wooden balcony, buttressed on all sides by oak beams that would take decades of rot to remove. It was no showroom, but neither would it have been an eyesore in its day. Both men were told to arrive alone, but neither was anything of the kind. Guards were stationed on the rooftops and in the alleys across the street, and even a skeleton crew had been installed in the upper balcony by each. Everyone had been instructed to remain out of sight, but none of them was doing it well.

Welliver surveyed the decay with evident derision.

"Let's transact our business and leave before the walls cave in, huh?"

Rolf at last looked up as if noticing his surroundings for the first time. The half-open eyes and perfume of port on his collar made that a distinct possibility. The eyes stared into nothing.

"...with half a stake, you're welcome to make any renovations you see fit. I'll not object."

Cy Welliver's eyes turned to slits as he sized up his conversation partner. "From the smell of you, you wouldn't object to much. The Long Moonlight givin' you a case of the vapors?"

Eghenston stepped over the sleight as if encountering a dead man in the road.

"In any event. A neutral venue."

Welliver clicked his tongue and gave a slight nod, placated by the conciliatory gesture.

"Aye then. Let's have it."

Rolf assembled his best befuddled expression and then replied for the sake of continuing the discourse. "…are we agreed we benefit little, if at all, from continued clashes in the streets?"

"Has the ring of truth to it," Welliver agreed with a grumble. "Though I'm still waitin' on a real reason for me to give up my gains in the Kallas and Royal districts. Seems fortune is breakin' more my way than yours."

"…and would that extend to the entire southern portion of the Gylvain? Which now swarms with my men?" Rolf retorted with the barest semblance of composure. "As I recall, those were your numbers rackets and dice parlors not a week ago."

Welliver's eyes rolled. "You're a hard man to wisecrack with when you're 'faced."

"You'll find even while sober, I'm amused with some difficulty."

"Like a priest with no pockets."

"I… don't understand."

Welliver shrugged, "I came for a meeting, not a miracle."

"Then we've come to the primary purpose of our conference." Rolf steadied the conversation with a jerk. "I have no objection to restoring the previous boundaries. Flawed as they were even before our current… difficulties. And in exchange…."

Welliver's anthracite eyes followed Rolf's hand as it suddenly raised, palm flattened, fingers outstretched. Asking for something.

"Are you… going to do something with that?" Welliver asked, quizzically.

Eghenston's gaze leveled itself. Directly at Welliver.

"Let's not be pedantic, Cy. Not at this late juncture."

Cyrus Welliver's eyes shrank to obsidian slits. Knowing eyes. The kind that saw secrets and kept them. So long as they were his.

"…come again?" he purred.

With those two words, Rolf Eghenston was suddenly sober.

"The pearl."

Almost before he'd finished the words, a guardsman's scream rent the night air. Both bosses craned their necks upward in time to witness a tumbling figure, hurtling to the floor from the upper balcony. It was spared the fatal impact, an arrow through the eye ending his suffering before he hit the ground. He was one of Welliver's guardsmen, knocked from his perch by ambush.

With one arrow, the stalemate was ended.

Cyrus Welliver drew a dagger the size of a short sword from his boot and spat through clenched teeth, "Even this late in the game, I told myself I'd never again be surprised by your treachery, Kinslayer..."

Rolf removed a walnut-hilted dirk concealed in the breast of his doublet.

"...so it was boon trust that led your men to crouch on the balcony like heavy-footed hitmen?"

"For your throat's sake, get used to heavy feet," Welliver growled and lashed out with his massive blade. Rolf blocked and spun, shouting to the rooftops all the while:

"BRECKEN! DOM! Boys! To me!"

Rolf struck back at Welliver while his men were working their way down from the balcony. Opposing forces delayed them. Only Brecken broke through the blockade, ears tuned to the sound of dagger on halfsword, he bounded through the double doors in time to catch the hulking crimelord looming over his employer, overpowering him in a clash of blades.

An object whistled overhead. It sank with a sick thud into Brecken's chest, cracking his hardened leather chestpiece in half. An arrow had impaled his sputtering heart.

The lanky tough muttered an impotent oath as he sprawled on his deathbed.

Outside, the sounds of struggle drew forces from each side to join the bloodletting. Sword met shield, mace met flesh, and axes were drawn in the Long Moonlight. It was less a battle than a riot, as the cobblestones teemed with hired killers bent on open slaughter and succeeding.

Inside, the crimelords fed on the carnage, Cy Welliver's eyes were wide with murderous intent, and Rolf assumed the savage countenance of a rabid timberwolf. They lashed in turn, each wounding the other, openly bleeding from a half-dozen gashes within just the first few moments of the duel's beginning. Welliver boasting by far the greater bulk... but Rolf well surpassing his skill with a sword.

Another object hissed overhead, illuminating the Night Gallery as it flew. Soared. Sunk into the dry timber of the balcony buttresses. Between the parched air, the sawdust, and the rotting beams themselves, the fiery missile was well on its way to setting the entire north balcony alight within moments and already had its eye on the arched ceiling.

The pressure soon blew the windows out with a terrific explosion.

Hapless henchmen outside the Night Gallery looked upward for a moment and were rewarded with swift decapitations by their opponents. Yet they had been looking in the wrong direction.

For at that moment, from the opposite side of the street, a single sentry advantaged with a longbow shrieked and doubled over the roof's edge, slumping into the street below. An arrow was once again the culprit. The fletching showed the blue plumage of the City Guard.

"FIRE!" a voice shouted, seeming to emanate from all directions at once.

From the rooftop of a hotel opposite the west edge of the Night Gallery, a sea of bowmen bearing the insignia of the City Guard leapt to their feet and fired a full volley upon the warring gangmen below. At their head, sword drawn and directing the attack, was Inspector Coggins. Inscrutable eyes combed the criminal hordes.

The tip from his mysterious thief informant had proven true.

The criminal swordsmen fled in terror, lacking any offensive recourse, as their own sparing accompaniment of archers was already nearing depletion.

In the blazing Night Gallery, the twin combatants were unpersuaded. Their better logic subsumed by bloodwrath, even the calculating Eghenston had come unhinged. He slashed sideways at Welliver's bulk. Arcing bloodspray shot from the edge as the blade came free. The giant did not yield. Rolf having been carried by the momentum of the merciless blow, he had made himself vulnerable. Welliver did not miss the opportunity. Shoulder-blocking his foe backward into an upturned table, he threw himself upon Rolf Eghenston. The cagey swordsman anticipated the action, and sidestepping with his blade directly ahead of his body, he let Welliver's heaving mass carry him forward.

Directly on to Rolf Eghenston's swordpoint.

The anthracite in Cy Welliver's eyes blazed, cooled, and finally, extinguished.

The mammoth crimelord collapsed forward, crushing Eghenston beneath him, blade still buried in his stomach. As he fell, the tip of the dirk erupted from the other side.

Eghenston fought the rapidly spreading fire for the remaining air and desperately sought a way to unpin himself from his dead enemy's cyclopean corpse.

"You were right, Rolf."

He heard a voice say, faintly, in the balcony above. Following the sound, he saw a lone, hooded figure, longbow relaxed in his left hand, leg propped on the edge of the burning balcony. Just beneath the edge of the hood, he thought he spied a splash of cobalt warpaint splayed across the man's eyes.

His mouth pulled in a self-satisfied smirk.

"...just because a man has much doesn't mean it's enough," Xerdes finished.

Eghenston's eyes bulged as he vainly attempted to roll the lifeless behemoth off his rapidly suffocating body.

"Anything, Xerdes!" he choked, praying it was audible above the blaze. "Gold! Narcotic operations! Your own bloody district, lad!"

The figure above him chuckled darkly.

"Haven't you heard...?"

With that, he reached beneath his long, flowing cloak and withdrew a single gray pearl, whirling with a spectral mist at its center. Then, to Eghenston's astonishment, he paused. And produced another.

"...I'm the richest man in Menuvia."

Coggins swept through the halls of the City Guard at a dizzying pace. Huddled around stacks of parchment and desk lamps, it seemed all of headquarters craned their necks to follow the inspector's indefatigable advance. Though the fire at the Night Gallery still raged and his men were still pursuing the survivors, Coggins had other business to attend, leaving it to subordinates to round up the remaining offenders as he rushed off with little explanation. Word had already reached of his swift rout of the criminal hordes. Word had also spread of how many guardsmen, none of whom had come with Coggins, were found among the deceased. Reaching the end of the great hall, he observed Captain Bevens, looking apoplectic as usual, alongside a man in a smart, midnight blue uniform. The ornate v-shaped insignia that swept from shoulders to stomach said he was not of the Guard, but the Menuvian military. He greeted Coggins with a yellow grin and mustache akimbo. He had a kind face, if oblivious, and a solid mane of pale gray hair that was punctuated by a prominent bald spot. His advanced years and bent physique said he fought most of his latter-day battles with a pen and inkwell.

He halted Coggins's advance with a cannonade of praise.

"Lieutenant Coggins!" he bellowed, extending a white gloved hand in commendation. "General Krenwick, Inspector. Hearing the tale, I couldn't help but rush down for a personal introduction."

Coggins brought his fist laterally across his chest in a smart salute, but said nothing. The General spoke for the both of them.

"Now, there's still some formalities to attend to. Committee approval, a senate signature, and the like, but barring any unforeseen circumstances, I'd say you're looking at special dispensation by week's end, son! Well d—"

Coggins had pushed past the general and Captain Bevens wordlessly. Recruit Friedrich blanched in horror when he saw it, having never witnessed such an act of abject disrespect in person. Eyebrows like oversized gray caterpillars furrowed in puzzlement as the General watched him pass. Sparing a quick look for Captain Bevens, he stiffened his lip, shrugged, and pursued Inspector Coggins at a surprisingly sprightly pace. Coggins did not look back but pressed on through winding hallways, past armories, and an indoor archery range. His pace began to slow as they arrived at the offices of the City Guard.

He came to a particular door, spun on his back heel, and stated coldly,

"I would be obliged if you would open this."

Captain Bevens pressed the edges of his uniform and gave the General a pale glare. General Krenwick seemed lost in the sport of it all.

"Jove!" he exclaimed, "I'll do it if only to see what this is all about, Lieutenant." With that, he felt for his keyring, fumbled with it while Bevens looked on, and opened the office. The three crowded inside while the General's curiosity at last gained the upper hand.

"What exactly is all this about, Lieutenant?"

"The pearl heist, sir." Coggins said, taking a knee and bending over a footlocker against a far wall beside the desk.

"Yes?" Krenwick said, mustache bristling beneath a bulbous nose as he did. "I thought we'd put that down to the same criminal element you almost single-handedly purged just this evening."

"Factually assessed," said Coggins clinically. He wasn't finished. "Yet incomplete. After a nearly successful heist seven years ago, one-way gates were installed at the base of the Spire."

"Oh, yes," Krenwick said, nestling his chin in his hand as he did so. "With the lock only on the inward side."

"Precisely. So as to be made impenetrable to even the most adept picklock. It can, in short... only be opened by an inside man."

The general's face wrinkled like a wet bulldog.

"Yes, we've a problem with guardsmen being tempted by men of greater money and lesser morality and no mistake."

"—a problem we have pursued aggressively, sir," interrupted Captain Bevens. "There are twenty-five officers awaiting indictment as we speak."

The General nodded in placation. Coggins did not join him.

"The one-sided gate was not the only security measure installed seven years ago. We also entrusted the key to no one below the rank..." his eyes locked upon Bevens for the first time since arriving. "...of Captain."

Krenwick bristled uncomfortably, ankle-deep in the thickening atmosphere. Coggins produced a lockpick from beneath his uniform and went to work on the foot locker.

"Lieutenant, explain yourself this instant!" shouted the Captain, abandoning his artifice of austerity. There came a click. Coggins pulled the lid aside gently.

Within was a pale gray orb, its innermost depths swirling hypnotically with an eerie ivory ether. The general's brow lowered, shadowing his eyes. His voice sank to a barely audible, solemn intonation.

"Inspector," he said. "whose locker is this?"

Coggins peered past his shoulder.

Past General Krenwick.

Past Captain Bevens.

A blade came free with a musical sheen. Behind Bevens, from the doorway beyond, pounced a trembling, sweat-sopped, nervous figure, wild eyed and manic, deep sable curls dangling before his dripping, olive brow. Recruit Friedrich held Captain Bevens at sword point.

"N-now listen!" his voice cracked in nervous fits, unable to control the volume. "I-I opened it. I... but I w... I was asked to! I don't h-have a k-key! No recruit g-gets a key. You just said it! You know that!"

The General held his hands out in a supplicative gesture. Coggins did not move.

"...and who, son?" started Krenwick. "Who hired y—"

Another blade joined the fray. This one ripped from Captain Bevens's waistband, turning. Twisting. Directly into the neck of Recruit Friedrich, spurring a terrific fountain of blood that showered Bevens' forehead. The sword slipped from the recruit's grasp. He reeled, staggered, sank to the ground, and made a vain attempt to speak. A bloody, bubbling croak was all he could manage.

The confused, corrupted young boy died. Bevens watched him do it.

"Are... are you in the altogether, my good man?" General Krenwick asked Bevens. The captain nodded, still trembling from the infusion of adrenaline. "Who in the Rift could have made such a promising lad aid in the most brazen heist in history?"

Coggins's face was a mask.

"I suppose we'll never know," offered Bevens, his normally uncompromising baritone reduced to a ragged rasp. Shallow. Panicked.

He spun awkwardly, gave one shuddering glance to the pallid body bleeding out on the floor beside him, and exited the office.

Coggins's eyes followed the Captain like a predator on open grassland. His gaze was cool. His mind was calm. His thoughts turned quickly, precisely, deliberately as the wheels of a threshing machine.

Clockwork and ice.

———————————————————

A burning portion of ceiling smacked the floor between the two men, having no effect other than to complement their conflagrant discourse.

Seeing two of the Pearls of Härdöval in the thief's possession, Rolf's normally unmoving, steel-grey eyes became a blast furnace. His pallid face swelled with hatred. He had no more honeyed words nor any more incentive to proffer them.

"You cur! Is that what this was about? Your pay?" He coughed and made another fruitless push. The sheer intensity of his antipathy allowing him to make the slightest headway. "I invested it in a grander future! One I invited you to join!! You need only have given—"

"I wouldn't give you the skin off an apple."

Eghenston went quiet, gave Welliver's corpulent carcass another push, and went back to the anvil.

"A life for a cut! Is a percentage not preferable to a life of worry? Dreading which shadow is a man and which of those holds a knife? I'm not an enemy you'd want to remake all over again..."

"What's two percent of nothing?"

Rolf's face went red while his hatred went white. He spat at the thief, knowing it would never reach.

"A death of your own devising waits for you, cutpurse! You're more mouth than man! A mewling, half-smart milksop cowering in corners, cocooned in shadows like an infant, delusory in the belief that the darkest secrets are ever hidden behind locks!"

Xerdes gave full flower to his smirk, scoffed, and turned to escape the actively collapsing conflagration. Errant embers already clung to the edges of his cloak.

"The only secret I needed... I already had."

The roof groaned in immolated misery. Xerdes took the cue and ducked out of a nearby door. Moments later, one entire half of the ceiling

collapsed in a cacophony of flaming rubble directly atop Rolf Eghenston and Cyrus Welliver, criminal rivals united in death.

The Night Gallery was their coffin and funeral pyre.

Xerdes ascended the side of the building but could not go down on that particular side due to the intensity of the fire. He ascended, instead, hoping to cut across the remaining section of roof and to descend on the opposite side. Below, he could hear the death agonies of the criminal cabal as they were hunted down like dogs in the street and executed by the City Guard.

Pulling himself over the edge of the roof, he came to the yawning pit where the ceiling had collapsed on the twin terrors of the Menuvian underworld. He stood upon the edge, flames lapping at the tips of his knee-high leather boots, and paused in deadly reverie. He unclasped the bag at his back and withdrew the two pearls, pondering the roiling fathoms of diaphanous ether within.

He looked deep in the core of the coveted orbs.

He saw nothing at all inside.

One at a time, the Pearls of Härdöval slipped from loose fingers and plummeted headlong into the flames. He let them fall.

After what seemed like laboring minutes, he sent the bag of Rolf Eghenston's blood money to join them.

He swallowed. It was like pouring a thimble full of water on an open desert.

Xerdes dared not delude himself into believing he'd done anything on behalf of the innocents they'd slaughtered. Not even had he believed innocents existed. He didn't indulge the self-deception that it was even for Saryss, carved like a fish and pinned to his tenement window. He knew none of it was permanent. By morning, the murderers would have new masters. The same children would get on the same meatwagon and wind up in the same bedchambers with the same sneering deviants. The same palms would get the same grease. Only the money would land in a different pocket. There was nothing so adaptable as avarice and nothing so ephemeral as justice.

"Justice." He shook his head at the word.

FANNING THE FLAMES

As the flame-ravaged roofbeams popped and crackled about him and the unmistakable, acrid stench of roast flesh overcame even the oppressive heat of the inferno, Xerdes watched and to his dismay, found himself admiring the sight. He did not linger on the macabre sensation.

Shafts of sunlight were already peeking from beyond the spires of the Menuvian skyline, the eyes of the city saturnine against the sunrise. The Long Moonlight fled before it.

Xerdes vaulted from the roof and vanished into the dawn.

Xerdes will return!

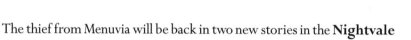

The thief from Menuvia will be back in two new stories in the **Nightvale** series from RazörFist and Dark Legion Books!:

- *The Ghost Wind*

- *The Faceless Phantom*

Lightning Source UK Ltd.
Milton Keynes UK
UKHW010227201120
373723UK00001B/73

9 789527 303092